A DEBT TO PAY

A Western Frontier Adventure

◇

Robert Peecher

For information the author may be contacted at

PO Box 967; Watkinsville GA; 30677

or at mooncalfpress.com

This is a work of fiction. Any similarities to actual events in whole or in part are purely accidental. None of the characters or events depicted in this novel are intended to represent actual people.

Copyright © 2019 ROBERT PEECHER

All rights reserved.

ISBN: 9781795863155

FOR JEAN

CONTENTS

Chapter 1 ... 1

Chapter 2 ... 21

Chapter 3 ... 33

Chapter 4 ... 50

Chapter 5 ... 61

Chapter 6 ... 74

Chapter 7 ... 82

Chapter 8 ... 92

Chapter 9 ... 103

Chapter 10 ... 113

Chapter 11 ... 126

Chapter 12 ... 132

Chapter 13 ... 149

Chapter 14 ... 158

Chapter 15 ... 162

Now a promise made is a debt unpaid,
and the trail has its own stern code.

"The Cremation of Sam McGee"
By Robert W. Service

- 1 -

Teresa called her last name Hogan even though there'd never been a preacher to speak words at her and Red.

In a mountain cabin where the nearest neighbors were in a hollow on the other side of the western hills, the talk of preachers gave way to common practice. Teresa figured the one hundred dollars Red Hogan paid for her in a Las Vegas brothel were just as good as any words a preacher might recite. Either way, she belonged to Red, so she took his name.

Though she was already five months along and her swollen ankles and back ached, Teresa was out in the garden when she heard a horse that wasn't one of theirs.

She peered through the deep forest of tall pines, but she saw nothing there.

Nonchalantly, Teresa picked a few more strawberries, dropping them into her upturned apron, and then walked unhurriedly back into the cabin. Her relaxed manner was a show for whatever man belonged to the horse she'd heard.

The dirt floor was cool beneath her bare feet. Candles provided the only light inside the dark cabin. When Red built the cabin he put windows in three of the walls and a door in the fourth, but now the shutters were all closed and only the tiniest amount of light came in through the cracks.

"Red, I heard a horse in the woods," Teresa said.

Red Hogan was stretched out on the mattress where he and Teresa slept.

Since they'd come into the Santa Fe Mountains at the southern end of the Sangre de Christo, almost two years ago all he had done was work. He felled trees and planed them and hauled logs and cut them and built a cabin. He made a fireplace out of stones he hauled up from the river. He did not have a plow, so he used a hoe to cut out a garden. He built a corral in the meadow clearing where he kept the horses and cows. He built a coop for the chickens.

He planted seed and harvested from the garden and hunted deer and turkey. Sometimes he'd climb all the way down to the Pecos and catch a mess of trout.

The thing was, Red Hogan wasn't built for work like this. Some men were, but Red Hogan was not.

He'd made a living behind his six-shooter, and that had always bought him an easy sort of life. Holding up stagecoaches was Red Hogan's bailiwick. In a pinch he could rustle cattle or steal horses, but stagecoaches offered hard cash, and that's what Red liked.

For Red Hogan, there was not much better than busting open a strongbox and finding a shipment of silver coins.

But when a posse caught up to him at his cabin hideout in a rocky canyon west of Santa Fe a couple years back, it turned into a massacre. Red's gang knew the posse was coming. They hid among the high rocks and dry-gulched that posse.

They finished off that posse in something less than two minutes, and when it was done, a dozen lawmen and volunteer posse lay strewn on the white stones, shot all to hell.

Not long after, there didn't seem to be a wanted poster in New Mexico Territory that didn't have his name on it. So he paid a hundred dollars to the owner of a Las Vegas brothel, rustled up some cattle, and Red Hogan went into the mountains, figuring to hide as long as he needed.

"Red, did you hear what I said?" Teresa asked.

She reached a hand around to put it into the small of her back, and she stretched as she did it.

"I'm sore uncomfortable," Teresa said. "Did you hear what I said to you about the horse?"

Red Hogan narrowed his eyes at her in the candle light.

Maybe it was the pregnancy, and Red's worries over what would happen when the time came and he was the only one there to help her birth the baby. Or maybe it was just his ramblin' spirit calling to him. But Red was feeling a mite restless lately. His restlessness meant he was working less and napping more, and his pregnant wife was growing surly over it.

These days, there wasn't a thing she said to him that she didn't say at least twice.

"Red! I heard a horse outside."

"Oh, you didn't hear no such a thing," Red Hogan said, starting up from the mattress in a huff. "If that's a horse outside, somebody's more lost'n he knows."

Red fetched his gunbelt and strapped it on. He had to check to be sure there were cartridges in the cylinder. That was never something he had to do before. He used to always know for sure the condition of his guns, but living alone with Teresa in the wilderness had made him careless.

"I'll go and have a look," Red said.

He stopped at the door where he kept the scattergun. He picked it up and broke open the top. He took two shells from the sack hanging on the peg by the door and he loaded the gun.

"I ain't saying there's anything out there, but you keep this nearby just in case," Red told her.

The door to the cabin was a poor example of its breed. Three leather straps nailed to the doorframe and to the door served as hinges, and the door was crafted from boards Red hewed himself. They fit together poorly, and so he had fitted the door with two skins to keep out the cold winters.

Just beyond the cabin door was the vegetable garden and the meadow where Red had built a corral for the livestock.

Red scanned the meadow and saw nothing but his own horses and cows. At the opposite end of the meadow ran a small creek that fed into the Pecos River. The stream dropped through the forest, over a tall cliff, and then flowed down into the Pecos River in the valley below.

Both to east and west the mountains towered high over the little cabin.

No man would be here. Red Hogan knew that was true as he peered into the shadows cast by the tall pine trees.

Down below a rough trail cut through the valley following along the same path as the Pecos. In places, when the river cut a deep gorge, the trail ran on a high ridge. They were hard miles along that trail with steep inclines and rocky slopes, and a man on horseback would be hard-pressed to make it to the mouth of the valley less than two full days.

Far to the south, the valley emptied out near a stagecoach station, and the Pecos River continued its path south through the territory to its confluence with the Rio Grande in Texas.

The stagecoach station sat down in the pass that allowed folks to travel from Las Vegas to the east to Santa Fe to the west.

The Taos people sometimes traveled down through the valley. Sometimes Utes. It was rare that the Apache might come into the valley to hunt, but sometimes they did.

White travelers were even more rare. An occasional trapper or hunting party might follow the Pecos valley north into the mountains, but Red Hogan had never seen a white man stray up into his meadow. Not in the two years he and Teresa called this place home.

He did have one neighbor. Twenty miles away, or so, a man from Colorado who'd done some prospecting there had come down to New Mexico Territory with his wife and children and settled. There were probably others, too, maybe farther north and maybe some to the south. Men and women who preferred not to be around others. But if they existed, Red Hogan had never come across them, nor had they ever come across his place.

Teresa was the daughter of Spaniards who stayed in the territory after it became part of the United States. Raven hair and black eyes, brown skin that was smooth to the touch, she was a stunning woman. She was not much over seventeen when Red Hogan brought her up to the mountain hideout.

Red himself couldn't be more different. From his Irish blood he'd earned a crop of red hair and pale skin that burned easily in the summer sun.

Red walked out around the cabin, looking through the pines, stopping frequently to listen. He saw nothing and heard nothing. Still, it wasn't like Teresa to spook easily.

He started back around the cabin when he heard the horse blow, and Red Hogan went for his six-shooter.

"Don't do it!" a voice called through the shadows of the pines. "There's more than just my rifle already on you. We'll cut you down where you stand."

Easy, without making any moves that might lead an unseen man to get nervous, Red Hogan stretched his hand away from his boy.

A young man who couldn't have been much over two decades, came skidding down out of the woods. He wore a tall hat with a wide brim, the crown pinched at the front to make large dimples in the side. A badge gleamed on his vest. He was trying for a mustache, but only a shadow of the thing existed. He toted a Henry repeating rifle with its signature brass receiver gleaming in the afternoon sun.

The young man stopped while he was still well out of Red's reach.

"We got you covered, Hogan, so don't you try nothing," the young man said. Then he set the rifle down, leaning it against the trunk of a pine, and he eased around behind Red.

"Just keep them hands up over your head, Hogan," the young man said.

He reached around Hogan's waist and unbuckled the gunbelt and slid it off.

"Step away from him now, Buck," the first voice called out from the woods.

Now the man who'd spoken from the woods stepped out from behind the trunk of a tall pine and walked out of the shadows. Like the younger man, this one also carried a Henry. But the resemblances ended there.

The older man, this one in his late thirties, was hard worn. He sported a heavy mustache under his nose, and his cheeks were covered in growth that suggested it had been a couple of days since he'd seen a razor. His head gear was the woven straw sort worn by charros with a wide brim and a low crown. He wore a brown coat embroidered with fancy designs stitched in a lighter shade, and he wore his holster low on his thigh.

"Howdy, Compton," Red Hogan said to the man.

"Howdy, Red. Anybody else in the cabin besides the woman?"

"She's the only one."

"Best tell her to come on out of there with her hands empty," the man called Compton said. "She looked pregnant. I guess I'd rather not have to shoot a pregnant woman today."

Red Hogan nodded.

"Teresa!" he called at the cabin. "Leave that scattergun and come on around to the back of the cabin."

When Teresa came around the corner, the younger man already had Red Hogan's wrists shackled in front.

"Teresa, this here is Rick Compton. He's a deputy marshal. I don't know his friend, but I reckon he's a deputy marshal, too."

"My name's Buckner," the young man spoke up. "Folks call me Buck."

"Your name is Buck Buckner?" Teresa asked.

"Buck ain't my first name. It's just what folks call me, on account of my last name."

Teresa's face showed her confusion. She had not yet realized what was happening, though she knew that deputy marshals being at the cabin could not be a good thing. And then, taking in the scene, and seeing that Red's hands were shackled, Teresa's face flashed hot.

"What is going on here?" Teresa Hogan demanded.

"We're taking Red back to Santa Fe," Compton said to her.

"Red?" she asked.

"Ain't nothing to do about it," Red told her.

Compton moved over to Red Hogan and, holding

the heavy Henry rifle in one hand and taking the back of Red's collar in the other hand, he pushed and pulled Red over to a fallen tree not far from the back of the cabin.

"You sit here," he said. "Buck, you go check out the cabin and make sure there ain't nobody else in there. Give it a good search for weapons and bring those out."

The younger deputy started around in the cabin, but Compton called to him. "Buck – your rifle?"

Buck chuckled at himself and hurried over to where he'd leaned his Henry against a tree.

"Right," he said, picking it up with a grin. Then he continued around to the cabin.

"What about me?" Teresa Hogan said. "What am I to do?"

Deputy Compton looked her over.

"Ma'am, I have some sympathy for your condition, but I ain't here to chaperone womenfolk. We're here for the night and in the morning we'll leave out for Santa Fe."

Teresa looked to Red who was sitting on the log, looking a mite hangdog. He looked strangely older to her.

"Red?" she said, and a hint of panic was growing in her voice as she began to imagine a life here in the mountains with no friends, no family, and not even Red to help her.

Defeated, Red Hogan shrugged his shoulders.

"Ain't nothing for me to do about it," he said.

***

Deputy Buckner, the one who everyone called Buck, came out of the cabin with the scattergun and three rifles. Then he went back inside and came out with a basket full of knives – a couple of belt knives and four or five kitchen knives.

"That's all I found," he said to Compton.

Buckner stacked the guns on the ground a good ways off from where the prisoner sat.

"Watch the prisoner and the woman," Compton said.

He went into the cabin and spent several minutes. Outside the cabin they could hear him inside roughly searching the place. He was scattering cookware and overturning furniture. Buck had made no appreciable noise when he searched the cabin.

When Compton came out, he had found two more six-shooters and a pocket gun, and he was angry.

"Look here, kid – this is how you get us killed," Compton said. "You understand me? That there red-headed sonuvabitch settin' on that log is a no-account killer and thief. When you walk into his home you don't treat it nice like you're visitin' the preacher for Saturday supper. You don't go in there and look around. You go in there and search it."

Compton kicked a mushroom all to hell to emphasize his point.

"You search it. You understand me?"

Buck nodded, his face hot from being chastised.

"I understand."

Rick Compton shook his head.

"Now go and fetch the horses," Compton said.

Red Hogan looked up. "Wait a minute," he said. "It ain't just the two of you, is it?"

Compton grinned at him.

"Two of us, Red. Me and some tenderfoot deputy was all it took to bring you in. How's that make you feel?"

Red Hogan dropped his head again.

"That's right, Red," Compton said, a self-satisfied grin spread across his face.

Deputy Buckner returned a short while later with two saddle horses and a pack horse.

"Can I go inside and sit down?" Teresa asked.

"No," Compton said. "I ain't taking any chances. Anybody goes inside that cabin and I shoot them."

"Can I at least have a chair?"

Compton nodded to Buckner. "Go in and get her a chair."

"With a cushion," Teresa said.

Buckner fetched a chair and cushion from the cabin, but it sure didn't feel like deputy work to do it.

He set the chair down at the edge of the garden under the shade of a tall pine tree. The day was not overly hot, but the sun could warm a body up in a hurry.

"Ma'am, you want to come take a seat?"

Buck walked up to where Teresa was standing and watched her as she walked past the stacked weapons. All the guns were unloaded, but Buck knew women could be impulsive, especially Spanish women. He'd once seen a Mexican prostitute stab a man in the eye with a knitting needle when the man refused to pay for her services.

Buck, the oldest of six children, also suspected that pregnancy contributed to impulsiveness in a woman, and so he stood between Teresa and the weapons.

As she stepped around the cabin, Teresa's foot landed on a rock and she stumbled.

Deputy Buckner reached out and caught her by the elbow and put a hand in her back to support her.

"Gracias, deputy," she said, and then she smiled at him. "You are very gracious."

Buckner smiled and helped her the rest of the way to the chair.

"Would you mind getting for me a cup of water?" Teresa asked, and she nodded to the rain barrel.

Buck filled the dipper with water, replaced the wooden lid and handed the dipper to Teresa.

"You're very kind," she said.

Out front of the cabin now, they could not see Compton and Red Hogan.

"I do not know what I will do if you take Red from here," she said. "A pregnant woman, alone in these mountains. I will not have much of a chance."

Buck did not know what to say.

"It ain't none of my business, ma'am," he told her.

"Buck, come and get these horses, collect these weapons, and let's make a camp for the night," Compton called to him.

Compton and Red Hogan came around the side of

the cabin, Compton still keeping that Henry rifle pointed at Red's back.

The work of tending to the horses and making a camp all fell to Deputy Buckner.

He brushed them down and turned them out in Red Hogan's corral. He made up a fire outside and set a pot of coffee on to boil. He found meat in Red's makeshift smokehouse and fried it up with onions and potatoes recently taken from the garden and made a meal for all four of them.

Deputy Compton only moved to get himself a chair out of the house. Otherwise, he just kept the Henry rifle on his lap and he watched Red Hogan, sometimes taunting him.

"You know, Red, if you wanted to try something that would be all right with me. That basket with them knives in it. Maybe you should go for one of them knives. Or maybe you've got a pocket gun I overlooked inside the cabin. Whatever it is you're thinking of doing to try to come at me, it would be all right with me if you did it."

Compton also talked of the posse's massacre at the canyon hideout.

"I had a cousin riding in that posse. You know, I've heard you said if a man didn't want to be shot he shouldn't join a posse riding after you. Well, here I am. You going to shoot me, Red?"

Red Hogan did not respond to the taunts.

It was true enough that Red sometimes missed his life before these mountains and this woman. Teresa had a way of exhausting him. The work exhausted him. But Red Hogan had made a promise to himself that he wouldn't go back to that life. He found that promise hard to keep with Rick Compton mouthing off at him, but there wasn't nothing Red could do about it now.

After supper, Compton conceded to let Teresa go inside the cabin to sleep in the bed. He only agreed to the concession after Teresa submitted to having her ankle shackled to the bedframe.

They also did a more thorough job of incapacitating Red Hogan.

They laid him on his back by the corral and then tied his handcuffs to the bottom fence post so that his arms were up over his head. Then Compton tied his ankles together with a rope.

The deputies took turns staying awake through the night. They kept the fire going to provide light, Compton did not worry that they were diminishing a pregnant woman's supply of firewood.

***

Come morning, Buck made up a breakfast of smoked meat and eggs, and after they ate, he got the horses ready.

"You care which one I pick for you to ride?" Buck said to Red Hogan.

"The sorrel there," Hogan said. "It's the oldest of my horses. Might as well leave Teresa with the best."

They'd untied him from the fence post, and Red Hogan did not know his arms could be so numb and painful all at the same time. Some of the life had come back into his limbs during breakfast, but he was still terribly stiff. He'd not slept well, either, and morning found Red Hogan feeling a mite grumpy.

Buck saddled three horses and packed the pannier on the pack horse.

"We're two days from the stagecoach station," Compton said. "When we get there, we'll be most of the third day getting back to Santa Fe. The good news is that the jury tried you and the rest of your gang in absentia. You know what that means? That means you didn't have to be there to get a trial. You're already convicted, Hogan. In four days, you'll be swinging from the gallows."

Teresa Hogan heard all of this, and Red was miffed that her concerns had nothing to do with him.

"What about me?" she said. "You cannot leave me here alone. Can you not see that I am pregnant?"

Compton scoffed, grinning at her.

"It ain't my fault you decided to take up with the likes of Red Hogan. You come up into these mountains with a man like that, you shouldn't be surprised when one way or t'other you get left on your own."

Deputy Buckner listened to all of this and it made him feel sick to his stomach.

It had taken the two deputies more than two days to find Red Hogan's latest hideout.

An old trapper had come through Santa Fe with word that he knew where Red Hogan was hid out. The marshal offered the trapper reward money if he'd lead deputies, but the trapper demurred. For something less than the full reward, he drew a map.

The map was accurate to a point, but even with a mostly-accurate map, it took the two deputy marshals a couple of days after leaving the main trail to find the meadow and the cabin. And then they watched it for two full days and nights. Compton was worried that other members of Red's gang might be nearby in the mountains, and he wanted to be sure there would not be visitors when the time came to take Red Hogan into custody.

Teresa turned her pleas to her husband.

"Red, talk to them. Do not let them leave me here. I'm carrying your baby."

Red Hogan shrugged his shoulders and looked at the dirt.

"It's not that I don't appreciate your predicament, Teresa, but I ain't sure either of these deputies are much interested in the troubles of a pregnant woman."

Bitterly, Red Hogan glared at Deputy Compton.

"Ain't that right, Compton?" Red said. "The troubles of a pregnant woman don't mean nothin' so long as you get to hang her husband. If'n my child grows up with no daddy, that don't concern you none."

Rick Compton's face turned angry.

"On account of you, they's a whole lotta children growin' up without their daddies," Compton said. "It's hard to muster much sympathy for your pup or the bitch that's carrying it."

Red Hogan flinched at the insult.

"You're a brave man with a big mouth so long as my wrists are shackled," Red told him.

Buck finished with the pannier, listening the whole while to the others.

Red Hogan was a good bit older than Buck, up closer to Rick Compton's age. His wife, though – Teresa –

she wasn't any older than Buck. And the way Buck saw it, she'd not done a thing to deserve the troubles that were now upon her or the worse that would soon come her way.

"Maybe we ought to take the woman with us," Buck said to Compton. He said it under his breath. He knew better than to openly challenge the senior deputy.

"She ain't our problem, and you'd be best to forget about her now," Compton said. "She's a pretty girl, and I can understand how that plays on your sympathies, boy. But don't you forget that she's shacked up here with a known murderer – a highwayman who's killed good men."

Buck nodded. He wouldn't argue with Compton, and it would do no good to. Compton's mind was set, and he was in charge.

Buck braced Red Hogan as he climbed up into the saddle on the back of the sorrel, his wrists still shackled together.

Compton got into his own saddle as Buck handed up the reins to Red Hogan.

"Understand me, Hogan," Compton said. "You try to ride off and get away from us, and I ain't going to chase you. I'll shoot you in the back and kill you. You've already been convicted and sentenced to die, so I got no qualms on it."

Red Hogan grinned at him.

"Only thing that surprises me is that you ain't done it already," Hogan said.

Teresa stood by the corral fence. Her belly was swollen and protruding, but not yet so enormous as it would be. All the same, she looked uncomfortable standing there.

"Teresa, gal," Red Hogan said. "Maybe this is all for the best. I wasn't never much of a man for settling down, and cabin life was already starting to wear thin on me."

Teresa offered him a sad smile. But she was not crying. She seemed to accept her fate for what it was.

"I appreciate the kindness you've shown to me in these last couple of years, and I'm glad you're carrying my child. I hope you can manage to give the thing a decent life."

Red cleared his throat, and Buck thought the outlaw's eyes looked watery.

"There ain't much I can offer you now," Red said. "Except for one last kiss."

"Keep away from him," Compton said as Teresa started to step toward Red.

"Oh, come on Rick," Buck said. He was still standing beside his horse and had not yet gotten into the saddle. "It's just a kiss."

Compton's horse did a little dance and he touched the reins to the horse's neck to bring it back around.

"I'll watch 'em and make sure she doesn't slip him anything," Buck said.

"One kiss," Compton said angrily. "Make it quick, and she keeps her hands out where you can see them."

Buck nodded to Teresa. She held her hands out, palms exposed, and walked over to Red Hogan's sorrel. He leaned far over and whispered something in her ear. Whatever he said was fast, and Deputy Buckner could not hear it.

Then, quickly, he kissed her on her lips.

Teresa stepped back.

"I never loved you Red," she said. "But I thought you could give me a better life than pirooting above a saloon. I was not wrong about that, and you have. I'll not forget you. If it's a boy I'm carrying, I'll do everything I can to be sure he doesn't turn out like his father."

Red hung his head.

"Yep. That's probably for the best. Good luck to you, Teresa."

Compton took the lead on Red Hogan's horse and started off across the meadow toward the trail that would take them down to the Pecos River.

Buck nodded to the woman.

"Can I get word to anyone for you?" he asked.

Teresa shook her head. "If I had anyone in this world, I would not be here."

She did not cry nor plead. She was angry. She might also have been worried. But Teresa bore it with a stoic resignation, as if this was just another hassle in a line of them that she'd have to face as it came.

"I'm sorry to leave you like this," Buck said.

"I know you are," Teresa said. "I can see it in your eyes. You do not have a lawman's eyes. You should find another line of work."

Buck shrugged and shook his head.

At his feet was a blanket with all of Red's firearms tied in it.

"I'll drop this about a mile down the trail," Buck said, hefting the blanket full of guns. "By the time you get to it, we'll be well on our way."

Teresa raised her eyebrows.

"It's an unnecessary precaution," she said. "As far as I care, he's already hanged."

Deputy Buckner climbed into the saddle and set the blanket of firearms across his thighs. He tipped his hat to the pretty woman.

"Ma'am," he said, and he gave his dapple gray a touch with his heel to get it moving.

- 2 -

"I hope you boys know what you've got yourselves in for," Red Hogan said as they descended along the trail that wound its way down into the bottom of the Pecos valley. "The name Red Hogan offers folks some powerful strong feelings. You might find the most difficult part of hanging me isn't the catching me but the bringing me."

Red gave a laugh.

Rick Compton did not respond. They'd been riding for the better part of an hour, and Red Hogan had hardly stopped talking. Deputy Compton, leading the way down the trail, did not respond to anything Red had to say. It was all just idle talk. But Deputy Buckner didn't mind the conversation. His stomach was in knots over leaving that pregnant woman to whatever fate befell her, and the conversation helped to keep him from thinking about it.

"I have a feeling we'll be all right," Buck said cheerfully.

"Powerful feeling, Deputy Buckner," Red repeated. "Might be any number of folks who want to take a shot at me as we go riding past."

Buck grinned and gave a little chuckle.

"Well then, I hope their aim is true because I'm the one riding behind you."

Red Hogan laughed appreciatively.

"And, of course, you might have to worry about the Old Bunch," Red said.

"Is that your gang?" Buck asked.

"That's them. The Old Bunch. Hugh was the leader of the gang. And there were the brothers, Rusty and Dick Hale. And then me and Al. We was quite the outfit."

"Is that Hugh Bentley?" Buck asked.

"One and the same," Red Hogan said. "Hugh Bentley and I started riding together more than fifteen years ago. He might have a real interest to learn you've caught me and are bringing me in."

"He won't give us anything to worry about," Buck said.

"Why is that?"

"Hugh Bentley was rustling cattle last spring down south and he was shot by a posse. They hanged him on the spot."

Red Hogan fell silent for several moments.

"Dang. I didn't know that."

"Al Simpson was hanged in Carson City, Nevada a few months back," Rick Compton said.

Red Hogan let out a big laugh.

"Well, there's some good news. I never did like Al Simpson," Red told them. "I guess the Old Bunch is turning into the Dead Bunch, ain't we."

"Be one less soon enough," Rick Compton muttered.

"Still, if you think Rusty and Dick Hale can't scrounge up some gun hands to come give you trouble, you've got a poor notion of who you're dealing with."

"Nobody knows we come up here for you," Deputy Buckner said.

"Is that right?" Red asked.

"We learned you was up in these mountains, and Deputy Compton and I come to fetch you without telling anyone what we were doing."

"How'd you find out I was up here?" Red asked. It was a question that had been nagging at him.

"An old trapper found your cabin. Came to town and told us about it."

Some months ago Red had seen some traps set out a couple of miles from the cabin. He never saw any evidence that whoever set them had come as high up as the cabin, but it now made sense.

"You think that trapper hasn't said anything to anyone else?" Red asked. "I guarantee you that if you knew I was up in these mountains plenty of other folks have heard about it, too."

As they continued the descent down toward the Pecos where they would pick up the trail south, Deputy Buckner's mind began to drift and he stopped listening to Red Hogan.

Teresa Hogan was in for a rough patch. Buckner had witnessed and remembered some of his own mother's pregnancies. With one of his sisters, a doctor ordered Buckner's mother to bed for the last two months of the pregnancy.

Even if the pregnancy ran along smoothly until the day of the birth, more difficulties would likely still be ahead.

Some births were more difficult than others. Buckner remembered his own mother's exhaustion following a birth. He did not have clear memories of all of them, but it seemed that his mother always spent a few days in bed before she felt like getting up. Yet the baby would need immediate care. And living in a remote mountain cabin was not a life conducive to a day or two of rest. Every day she would need to get chores done.

Buckner had heard some stories of women giving birth when they were alone in the wilderness. It surely was a thing that happened. But few of those ended happily for both mother and child.

"It'll be a small miracle if your wife and child survive," Deputy Buckner said out loud, interrupting whatever soliloquy Red Hogan was making.

"How's that?" Red asked.

"Your wife and child," Buckner repeated. "If they survive the birth, it'll be a miracle."

"Bah," Red Hogan said. "Women been havin' babies as long as I can remember."

"What's she going to do?" Buck asked.

"I can't say. She's a resourceful gal. She'll get along."

"Will anyone come to help her?"

"Nobody knows where that cabin is. Except the two of you and that trapper who told you about us. Unless he's planning to head back out to the cabin now that I'm gone, ain't nobody going to help her."

"Maybe she'll come out on her own. If she could get to the stagecoach station, she could get help."

"Maybe," Red said. "I doubt it, though. She's Spanish stubborn. I reckon she'll stay at the cabin. God knows she's never had it better than that."

"Even if she makes it through the pregnancy and birth, I don't reckon she and your baby is going to survive the winter," Buckner said.

Red Hogan's shoulders bounced up to his ears.

"My conscience is clear on that account," Red told Buckner. "You and Compton is the ones that left her alone up there. I ain't going with you by choice. If her survival is so all fire important to you, how come you did not make a case to bring her with us?"

Buck stopped talking about it then. He knew Red Hogan had a point.

Deputy Compton, if he was even listening, made no argument in his own defense.

The three riders continued down the trail, and now even Red had fallen silent.

***

The main trail south through the Pecos Valley had existed, probably, for centuries.

Farther north, deeper in the Sangre de Christo

Mountains, the Taos people inhabited an adobe pueblo that had been standing for hundreds of years before the Spanish ever came through here. The Taos and other mountain dwellers surely used this trail for trading and hunting.

Not many white men came this way unless they were hunting or trapping, but the mountain tribes still sometimes came down through the Pecos Valley, and the plains tribes sometimes went into the valley from the south to hunt.

When Rick Compton dropped down off the mountain trail that led up to Red Hogan's cabin, there was no question about finding the better, more traveled path through the valley. The trail to Hogan's cabin was just a deer path, but here the trail was wide enough for two horses to walk abreast and easy to see.

"I reckon this'll be my final trail," Red Hogan said. "What do you figure, Compton? We about forty miles to the stagecoach station?"

"About that."

"Take us the rest of the afternoon and most of tomorrow," Red mused. "It ain't an easy trail in places."

"We'll find a clearing close to sundown and camp by the river tonight. We'll camp at the relay station tomorrow night," Rick said.

"You on alert for ambush?" Red asked.

"You still worried about that?"

"I have reason to worry, and you do, too."

"Nobody knows we're up here," Deputy Compton said with confidence. "And if they did, they'd be unlikely to try something. Folks want to see you walk up the gallows, Red."

"Lots of folks want me dead for lots of reasons, Compton. I reckon most will be satisfied if the hangman does it. But there may be some who would kill you to be able to be the one to puts a bullet in me. Don't you forget that."

They kept on a ways farther.

The flat bottom of the valley with the Pecos running along gently beside them made for a pleasant ride. Buckner could see the appeal of a place like this. He understood what drove a man to come here to make a life. If you could do without other people, it might be nice.

In a daydream, Buck envied Red Hogan's existence for the past two years.

A beautiful young wife and a cozy enough cabin. Red's meadow opened up the view of the peaks opposite, and in the wintertime, all capped in snow, those mountains must surely be majestic. The smell of pines was one of the sweetest smells Deputy Buckner ever knew, and here in these mountains, pine wasn't just a smell but it was the air itself. The Pecos ran clear and fast.

Between the deer and elk and trout, a man could never go hungry, and Red Hogan had a two-year garden.

In his mindless wanderings, Buck found himself living in Red Hogan's cabin. He saw the pretty, young woman smiling at him. Calling him by name.

"Buck, supper's ready."

He saw himself with young boys, his own children, casting a line in search of trout in the cool, clear Pecos.

Buckner felt suddenly transported into another life, a life that was not his own, but was also not Red Hogan's life. Red Hogan would never cast a line into the Pecos with his son.

"You ever think about Injuns?" Red asked, shaking Buck from his reverie.

"I think about 'em," Compton said.

"That might be a thing to worry about, too," Red Hogan said. "Injuns might throw up an ambush same as anyone else."

"You seen Injuns since you been up here?" Compton asked.

"I have. A time or two."

"They ambush you?" Compton said.

"Not yet," Red said.

"Well, they ain't likely to start today."

Compton's confidence aside, Buck started wondering if Red's warnings were idle talk or not. He kept his eyes on the ridges above them. At times, the pines were so numerous and the canopy so thick that he could see virtually nothing of the mountains overlooking the valley. But in other places, the river cut a wide enough swath, or the bottomland was open meadow, and there he could watch the hills above them.

He never saw more than a squirrel, but by the time they stopped to camp in a meadow near the Pecos River, Deputy Buckner's imagination was putting eyes in the hills and riders on the ridges.

"Buck, see if you can't catch us some trout," Compton said as they unsaddled the horses.

In addition to having him shackled, Compton took the extra precaution of sitting Red Hogan at the base of a tree and wrapping him up in a lariat.

"He ain't goin' nowheres, and we're getting low on provisions."

Buck had fished on the way up and caught a good mess of trout, and Compton took them as a delicacy. Not a fisherman himself, he said he didn't know that he'd ever had trout before.

When he was young, living back in Arkansas before coming to New Mexico Territory, Buckner had fished a lot with his grandfather. Those were some of his favorite memories. But fishing opportunities in New Mexico proved rare. So Buck greedily jumped at the task.

He waded into the knee deep river, casting his line just onto the surface where the trout would bite.

As he fished, his mind cleared of worries over Indians or dry-gulchers.

Several times when he looked back at the bank, he saw Red Hogan watching him.

Compton had little to do to make camp. Mostly he searched around for the right place to picket the horses so that each horse would have grass to graze and be able to reach the water.

He took some big rocks from the river and made up a pit for a fire and then collected firewood. Compton never left sight of the camp, and whenever Buck looked back to see what the older deputy was doing, he caught Compton glance up from his task to set eyes on Red Hogan.

The whole way up Rick Compton warned the

young deputy about Red Hogan.

"Red Hogan is as dangerous as they come. Once we have him in custody, you be alert to him all the time. Never take your eyes off of him. If you ain't watching him, you're giving him time to strike. And I guarantee you, if he ain't striking and trying to get free of us, he's plotting it." Compton repeated this warning, or some variation of it, over and over on the entire journey.

But they took him with such ease – no gunfight, and Red didn't even break and run – that Buck had to wonder if Compton's constant warnings weren't wasted breath.

Red Hogan didn't seem to have any interest in making a fight or going on escape. He was as meek and cooperative as a prisoner could be.

"That's three!" Buck called, pulling in another fish. "I'm gettin' out of this water afore I freeze my feet off."

The sun was descending fast and was already on the far side of the peaks to their west, casting everything around them in shadow. Buck knew it would take a bigger fire than the one Compton had going to warm his feet.

He walked up out of the stream and quickly cleaned the three fish on a rock.

Compton came over with the skillet from the pannier and handed Buck a cup of coffee.

"I reckon that water's a bit chilly," Rick said. "This'll help warm you up some."

"Let's get a couple more logs on that fire, too," Buck said. "We can scrape some of them coals to the side to give you something to cook on, but I'd appreciate some warmth."

Compton looked at the surrounding hills, but of course there was nothing to see.

"Not too big a fire," he said. "Warm yourself, but let the flames die fast."

"How come?"

Compton dropped his voice. They were standing well away from where Red Hogan was tied to the tree, but he still did not want to risk being overheard.

"If he's right and there might be Injuns in these hills, we don't want to build up a big fire that might show them where to find us. I'm already nervous enough that they'll smell the smoke."

Buckner hurried over to the fire to get his feet warm and dry before putting his socks and boots back on.

Buck cooked the fish, having more experience with fish than Compton, and Compton untied Red Hogan and moved him over by the fire. Red's hands stayed shackled, but for now he had freedom enough to feed himself.

"If you knew what you were doing, Compton, you'd make that fire, eat your dinner, and then move on about six miles," Red told him. "Only a fool would camp by his fire. Even after you kick dirt on it the smell of the smoke will linger for miles. If there's Apache in these woods, they'll smell it."

Compton growled at him.

"Did you ever have a fire in your chimney, Red?"

"I did."

"And did you then move your cabin six miles away?" Compton asked.

Red Hogan narrowed his eyes. "You're a fool Compton. That cabin was built up on a ridge. The smoke went high into the pines, the wind caught it and sent it off in every way. But we're down in the bottom of the valley here, and the smoke is just going to linger and set and invite every Apache with a scalping knife."

Compton didn't say anything, but Deputy Buckner heard every word of it.

They ate the trout and what was left of three-day-old biscuits.

After supper Compton kicked down the fire, and then the two of them put Red Hogan down on a bedroll near the base of a tree. They tied his hands to the tree so that he was forced to spend another night with his hands up over his head.

"We'll take turns on watch," Compton said.

"I'll take first watch," Buck said.

Maybe it was all the talk of Apache, but he was feeling restless.

- 3 -

Red Hogan woke with a start, and immediately felt the pain in his shoulders and arms. But it was not the pain that woke him. A horse blew and shifted its hooves nervously. Red held his breath, trying to listen for anything, expecting the worst at any moment.

He dared not speak.

Through the canopy above him he could see silver light. The moon was not full, but bright enough to break through the needled branches above him.

Red waited for his eyes to adjust, but even after a few moments he still could not see with any clarity anything around him.

Uncomfortable as he was, Red was not sleeping heavy. When the deputies traded out keeping watch, they woke him up. But he couldn't say if that had been ten minutes or two hours ago. Either way, Red knew that Rick Compton was keeping watch, and he was glad about that.

He heard another one of the horses make a

shuffling sound.

Whoever was out there making off with the horses was good at their business.

Red could have called out and raised an alarm. Like as not, that would have got all three of them killed. He did not care if the deputies were killed, but Red Hogan was defenseless. If they died, he would die right along with them.

Besides, even if there was not the threat of being murdered, what did Red care if the deputies had to walk him out? It might be hard on the legs, the days hot and the nights cold, but Red was living out his final days, and walking out of the mountains rather than riding out would prolong what life he had left.

Red listened close for several moments and then heard a horse snort. This was farther away now. Soon, whoever was taking the horses would be well away and clear.

But that horse snorting from a farther distance brought Compton to his feet.

Red Hogan could not see what was happening, but he could hear well enough as the deputy scrambled up and dropped the lever on his Henry rifle.

"Who's there?" Rick Compton called.

There was shuffling through the bed of pine needles on the ground. Compton cursing, and then shouting.

"Dammit! Buck! Hey, Buck! Wake up!"

Compton hurried back to where the bedrolls were laid out, and Red heard him give Buckner a soft kick.

"Buck, get up! Somebody's done stole our horses."

Now they were both awake. Buckner was out of his bedroll.

"Are you sure they're stole?" Buckner asked.

"Three of the four horses are gone," Compton said.

Buckner struck a match and lit a candle inside a lantern. He held it up high so that it cast an orange glow over the campsite. Red looked around.

The dapple gray that Buckner rode was still standing where the horses had been picketed. The other three were disappeared.

Buckner had his six-gun in one hand and the lantern held aloft in the other. Compton had the Henry rifle.

"Who the hell could have come into the camp and taken the horses?" Buck asked. "Didn't you hear them?"

"I didn't hear a thing," Compton said. "I didn't know anything until I heard one of the horses snort and realized it came from a ways away."

"Who could have done that?" Buckner asked again.

"Apache could do it," Red Hogan said.

"You keep your tongue, Red Hogan," Compton snapped, his tone full of anger.

"You think it was Apache?" Buck asked.

Compton didn't say anything. He held up a hand to quiet Buckner. He acted like he heard something. Red, watching from his bedroll, did not think there had been a noise.

"Go and get your horse and bring it over here to us," Compton said.

Buckner hesitated.

"You think anyone's still out there?" he asked.

"Take your gun. I'll cover you. Shoot at anything that ain't me."

Tentatively, Buck stepped toward where the horses had been picketed. He moved slow, keeping the gun out in front of him.

Red listened for any noise that might indicate the horse thieves were still there.

Anyone who made his living as a highwayman at one time or another also stole horses, and Red Hogan was no exception. He'd made some brazen getaways with other people's horses before, but he'd never seen anything quite like this. Whoever came in and took the three horses did it with a deputy marshal awake and on watch.

Red himself never heard a person, just the horses.

"That's a fine bit of horse thievin'," Red commented.

"Hush up, you," Compton said. "I'll cut your tongue out if you say another word."

Both deputies stayed awake for the rest of the night.

They kept the horse there with them in the middle of the campsite.

Red tried to sleep, but it was fitful and fruitless. Every time he would drift to sleep his arms would relax and new pains would shoot through his shoulders and wake him back up.

The most sleep Red Hogan got came just before dawn, and when the light of morning woke him up the deputies were already packing the dapple gray.

"We're walking out of here," Compton said. "It'll be another three, maybe four days. But there's nothing else to do."

"Could always take me back," Red suggested. "For the price of my freedom, I'd give you three horses from my remuda. You leave me at the cabin with Teresa, and you can ride on out of here."

"We didn't come up into these mountains to leave you here," Compton said. "We'll walk out together."

***

"Probably Apache," Red Hogan said.

Leading the dapple gray packed with their supplies, the three men had gone a couple of miles down through the valley. So far, the walk had not been arduous. The path of the river here was flat and there were wide, open spaces. Except that Buck and Compton were lugging the weight of their saddles on their backs, it was simply a pleasant stroll.

The birds were singing in the trees and the river made its own music as it rolled along. Beyond them, farther than they could now see, the river made a drop of some kind over a rocky shoal, and they could hear the current crashing against rocks. But Buckner had spent enough time on rivers that he knew sometimes a loud rapid did not necessarily mean a big drop.

Before this trip was over that river was going to

make some dramatic drops and it was going to carve out a canyon. The terrain was going to turn rocky, and they would have to climb ridges as the trail diverged from the stream. But for now it was pleasant enough, and Buckner hoped it would continue like this for some time farther.

"What'd you say?" Rick Compton asked. Buckner was glad to hear that Rick was breathing heavy. Buck worried that being the youngest he was the only one suffering on the hike.

"I said it was probably Apache," Red Hogan repeated, more loudly this time.

Red'd not kept up his running chatter so far this morning, but Buck guessed that pleasure was about to come to an end.

"A white man ain't coming into your camp like that and making off with your horses without making a sound. Dark as it was, that don't seem right. But an Apache, that'd be the thing to do for him. He gets to show off how skillful he is at horse thieving, and they love to do that."

Red paused for a moment to catch his breath.

In the last couple of years, Red'd done more hiking around in these mountains than he'd ever thought of doing before. And he was having an easier time of it than the two deputies because he'd abandoned his saddle rather than try to lug it out of the woods. But even so, Compton up front was setting a fast pace, and Red was running out of breath.

"The only thing that don't figure is why they didn't take our scalps, too," Red continued. "Surely there's more than three of them. And they had to know that I was bound, because they were surely watching us when we made camp. So they had numbers on us. And it ain't like an Apache to leave a scalp."

The shoals came into sight, and as Buckner had guessed, it was just a rock garden in the middle of the stream and there was only the slightest drop over maybe fifteen or twenty yards. Just a lot of rocks standing defiant against the current.

"Maybe they thought to take our horses one night and take our scalps the next," Red theorized.

"Dammit," Compton said irritably. "Do you ever stop talking? Did you talk like this when you was holding up stagecoaches?"

Red Hogan laughed.

"I'm on a deadline, Compton. Everything I got to say, I got to get it out now."

"I could use a drink of water," Buck called out from the back of their line.

Compton stopped and dropped his saddle down to the ground.

He stretched, raising his arms up over his head and working his shoulder where the saddle horn was resting. Buck, like a pantomime, did the same.

"I don't see why you boys don't just leave them saddles," Red Hogan said.

"Them horses was rented for us by city," Buck said. "But these saddles are our own. And saddles ain't cheap, Red."

Red laughed again. The more miserable his captors became, the more gleeful he was.

"I'll tell you one thing right now, boy. Every single

saddle I ever owned in my life came into my possession free of charge."

"I ain't a thief," Buck said. "I pay my way."

Red grinned at him. Delighted.

"Oh, I paid my way, too, son. And I'm still paying it. I just paid in something other than money. I paid in nervous glances over my shoulder. I paid in dirty, run-down hideouts. I paid in all them miles I run. And I paid in bullet holes. You know I've been shot four times? How many times you been shot?"

"You was not never shot no four times," Compton said.

"Sure I was," Red said.

He pointed to his inner thigh on his right leg just below his groin.

"Shot through and through right here," he said. "Cleaned it with whiskey, bandaged it with strips of torn shirt, and then got in a free saddle and rode like hell."

His hands were still shackled, so he thrust his right upper arm at Compton.

"Shot in the muscle right there in my arm. Tore me all to hell. But a doc down at Fort Craig dug that out and it healed right up."

Now he tilted his head so that the left side of his neck showed outside of his collar.

"You see that scar there?" Red asked. "You see it?"

"I see it," Compton said after a perturbed glance.

"That's where a bullet dug a trench out of me. Bled like the devil for two days, and the Old Bunch all figured I was dead for sure. But it healed up, too."

Now Red stepped closer to where Buck was standing, and he craned his head the other way, leaning it toward Buck.

"Feel the side of my head boy."

Buck reached out and ran his fingers over Red's head, just above his ear.

"No, now. Back a ways further," Red instructed.

Buck moved his fingers farther along toward the back of Red's head until he came to a hard bump about the size of a knuckle. Buckner recoiled in revulsion.

"What the hell?" he said.

Red Hogan brought his head back up laughing like the devil.

"That's bullet number four. You'll bury that one with me."

He brought his shackled hands up and touched the side of his forehead.

"You see that scar? That's where number four went in. Traveled right around the side of my skull up under the skin, and it just stayed right there behind my ear. Ain't that something? The Old Bunch all joked that they knowed I was hard headed."

That sent Red Hogan into spasms of laughter so that tears welled up inside of his eyes.

"The Old Bunch. They was something else. We had some big ol' times, I'll say that. Did a lot of running and had some hard times. But then we'd pull up in Las Vegas or Mora or Santa Rosa or Cochiti or some damn village not even worth a Spanish name, and they'd be a big fandango and we'd dance with the women and drink the mescal and spend every bit of our loot having ourselves a big ol' time for three or four weeks. Every pretty gal in the village would come to sit on our laps and we'd give them a gold coin or a pocket watch or a diamond stick pin to remember us by."

Red Hogan seemed transported. A smile on his face and memories gleaming in his eyes.

"Those were some days," Red said with a shake of his head. "We'd ride into a village and it was like we was the kings of New Mexico Territory. I bet no lawman has never felt that."

Red grinned at them.

"Look at the two of you. Sweatin' and luggin' them saddles. Riskin' your lives for nothing except a bunch of folks who don't care about you and won't appreciate you can watch me stretch a rope. Who's the fool Compton? You or me?"

Rick Compton took another drink from his canteen and then slung it back over his shoulder.

"Let's get ready to keep going," Compton said.

"Ah, hell. Who am I kidding? It warn't no Apache stole your horses. Apache would have taken your scalps along with your horses. Nope. "The more I think about the old days, the more I think stealing horses in the middle of the night like that is the sort of thing the Old Bunch would have done. Take men's horses in the middle of the night and force them to walk. And then after they've walked a while and are good and tuckered, ambush 'em. They're softening you up. Making you easy targets. They'll wait until you come along to a clearing where it'll be easy to get you. Or down in a canyon where there ain't no escape. You don't have horses to get away. They'll cut you down."

"Why not just kill us when they took the horses?" Buck asked.

"Dark the way it was, maybe they didn't know who was awake and who wasn't. They could get as close as the horses without being heard, but couldn't get no closer. Maybe they just wanted rattle you a bit. Let you know they're here and they can get close whenever they want."

Compton spat on the ground.

"Don't matter if it's your old outfit or if it's Apache. Ain't nobody gonna save you, Red."

"Ain't nobody trying to save me, Compton. It's the Old Bunch up in these hills, but they ain't here to save me. They're here to cheat the hangman."

***

Compton was setting a hard pace, and the terrain was beginning to shift on them. Buck struggled up a hill, and he could see up ahead that there was another hill coming as the trail left the bottoms of the river and rose up the side of the mountain.

He could hear Compton breathing hard, and even Red Hogan had stopped talking.

Buck had his saddle slung over one shoulder and was holding it with one hand, and he had the dapple gray's lead in his other hand. Buck realized he would be a mite slow to respond if Red Hogan made some sort of desperate attempt.

But Red seemed resigned to his fate. He wasn't complaining or arguing at all. He'd made no effort to make a run or fight back.

Buck stared at the back of his head, wondering what kind of man gets shot four times and then gives up when two deputies come to take him.

Shot in the inner thigh and he rides away. Shot in the neck and it bleeds so bad his partners think he's going to check out, but he comes back around. Shot in the head and he just totes the bullet around under his skin, laughing when people touch it and are horrified.

"Why ain't you tried to run?" Buck asked.

Red didn't respond immediately.

"I asked you how come you ain't tried to run," Buck said again.

"It's awful hard walking through here just now," Red Hogan said. "Maybe we'll save the talking for later."

"We come to take you to the hangman's noose," Buck said. "Deputy Marshal Compton done told you they already tried and sentenced you. So how come you ain't tried to beat it?"

Red Hogan stopped and turned to face Buckner. At first Compton did not realize that Red had stopped, and he was still headed up the trail.

Buck saw that there was something different in Red's eyes now. The jovial playfulness was gone. The grin wasn't on his face any more. His eyes were serious and seemed to burn with a fire.

Compton was still hiking up the trail, but Red Hogan and Deputy Buckner were standing stock still.

"I could get away any time I please," Hogan said. "I could take that gun away from you and shoot Compton in the back afore either of you even knew what was happening. You'll only hang me if I let you hang me. But I got my reasons for going with you, and you don't need to know what those reasons are."

And then, before Buckner could stop him or react, Red Hogan hooked the back of Buckner's ankle with his own foot and shoved a shoulder into Buck's chest. The young deputy toppled over backwards, landing on his saddle and knocking the breath out of himself. The horse pulled away from the commotion and backed up several paces.

While Buckner gasped for breath, Red Hogan dropped to his knees and slid Buck's six-shooter out of its holster. Red thumbed back the hammer and turned the gun to point it at Compton.

"Bang," Red said softly, and started grinning at the young deputy still gasping for breath. Then he laughed a couple of times and set the gun on Buckner's chest. "Just like that, boy. I'm free any time I want to be. Don't forget it. You take me only so far as I'll let you."

Hogan stood up and hurried up the trail to catch up to Compton.

Deputy Buckner caught his breath and took several long, deep breaths through his nose as he tried to recover.

Buck took the six-shooter from his chest and let down the hammer. He climbed to his feet, holstered the gun, and then walked down the trail to where the dapple gray was standing. Buck retrieved the lead and then went back and picked up his saddle.

Deputy Compton never broke stride and was now well ahead. Buck realized that Rick Compton didn't even know what had happened.

Buck felt humiliated.

Like it was nothing, Red Hogan had unmanned him and disarmed him.

Buck cursed himself under his breath.

"Stupid to let him get so close," Buck whispered angrily at himself.

He looked at Red Hogan's back and considered shooting him dead right then and there. And Buck knew some of that was anger at how easily Red had handled him, but some of it was also fear. If he'd done it once, so simply, Red might do it again. But next time it might be for real.

The trail kept climbing. It was not a steep slope, but it was a steady increase, almost imperceptible. Buck was having to push himself off of his own knees to keep going in places. The saddle seemed to be getting heavier, and Buck looked at Red Hogan, not toting any burden at all, with a fair amount of jealousy.

Here on the hillside the trail was more open. There were trees to their left going up the slope, but the drop to the right was more severe here. Except for the occasional tall pine, they were exposed to the sun on the river side, and it beat down mercilessly.

Deputy Buckner did not know how long they'd been walking. If it was two hours or six, time was imperceptible to him.

But the sun was overhead, so he figured it must be early afternoon.

Eventually the trail stopped going up the side of the mountain. They leveled out and could hear the river down below them as it dropped through its gorge.

Buck caught himself looking down on it several

times, thinking how cool it seemed down there. In this place, the river ran under a thick, green canopy with pines and scrub oaks growing all along the steep, deep banks.

The river down below was as pretty a sight as a man might see, Buck thought.

But up here it was hot and dry and tasted of dirt. Buck found the saddle was difficult to hang onto because of the sweat on his hand.

"There's a meadow up ahead," Rick Compton called back. "We'll take a rest there."

That was good news, Buck thought. He needed to set a spell, take a drink of water.

The meadow was a long, gradual slope going up the mountainside, until it was again covered in pines. Pretty little purple and yellow and white wild flowers mingled with the tall spring grass in the meadow, and Buck left the gray to graze some as he wanted.

"Look here," Compton said, dropping his saddle at the edge of the meadow where a couple of tall pines offered shade. "This is a good spot. We can rest here for a little bit and then get going again. We'll be three or four days getting to the stagecoach station having to walk it, but I'd like to keep up a strong pace as far as we can go."

Rick sat down on the saddle he'd dropped, and Buck dropped his saddle, too.

But he didn't sit down immediately. Instead he paced a bit to enjoy the freedom of not having the heavy burden on his back.

Red Hogan sat down on the bare ground and then laid back so that you could barely see him in the tall grass.

Deputy Buckner walked to the tree line, looking back into the forest they'd just hiked through. Mostly it was tall pines with an occasional hardwood that somehow managed to get enough light to survive. The woods were nothing like the ones he knew back in Arkansas that were so thick with underbrush that you couldn't get through them. A large sandstone boulder cropped up out of the middle of the forest floor about thirty yards from where Buck was standing, and he thought it looked like an ideal place to take a seat. But he needed to stay close to Red Hogan.

Buck cast his gaze through the meadow. It was pretty with its colors and the gentle breeze rippling the tall grass.

As soon as they dropped down out of the mountains there wouldn't be so many colors. Juniper green and sand brown. That was about all the rest of New Mexico Territory had to offer by way of color. But up here in the mountains it was all pretty, and Buck felt at home. Like when he went fishing with his grandfather back in Arkansas.

The only thing that was strange to Deputy Buckner was that there were no birds around here chirping. He figured they were all down by the river, but it was strange to him not to hear a single bird.

He walked a little ways into the meadow, looking at the trail in front of them.

"Looks like we're going to drop down off of this ridge and pick up the river again," Buck said.

"Set down and take it easy," Compton said.

A thing forward caught his attention, and Buck

peered at it. It was just inside the tree line at the opposite edge of the meadow.

"Hey, Rick. Come here and take a look at this," Buck said. "Ain't that the strangest damn thing?"

Compton pushed the cork back down into his canteen and set it down on the ground beside his saddle.

"This had better be worth me getting up to look at," he said.

He stood up and walked over to where Buck was standing.

"There's a rock in them woods there looks just exactly like a horse," Buck said.

"I'll be damned," Compton said.

Red Hogan sat up.

"It moved," Buck said, pointing at it.

That's when a rifle shot cracked the stillness of mountain meadow and echoed back and forth between the competing slopes cut by the Pecos River.

- 4 -

"Ambush!" Rick Compton shouted.

Deputy Compton drew his six-shooter and fired off a shot, but the trees on the opposite side of the meadow seemed to come alive with rifle fire. A volley that had to be at least six or seven rifles erupted in response to Compton's single shot. Buckner made for the safety of the tree line behind him. Remembering the big boulder he'd seen, Buck didn't stop running until he reached the boulder and had jumped around to the other side of it. And there he hugged the boulder like it was his lover, pressing his cheek against the coolness of it.

More rifle fire came from the opposite tree line, and Buck could hear the bullets ripping through the branches and pine needles above his head.

He did not know that Compton was shot in the first volley.

Buck only now drew his six-shooter from its holster and cocked back the hammer.

The range was too far, but the feel of the Colt

Army in his hand gave him some comfort. A gunsmith converted the Colt to accept cased cartridges by drilling through the cylinder, but the box of spare cartridges was on that dapple gray, along with Buck's Henry rifle, and the gray was headed back the trail the way they'd come.

Six shots was all he had, and Buck wasn't sure but it seemed like there must be a hundred men in the woods opposite the meadow.

Buck peered around the boulder to try to get his bearings.

The boulder sat downhill from the meadow, not much, but it meant that a man standing at the opposite tree line was all but impossible to see from his position.

Rick Compton was on the ground and not moving.

"Rick!" Buck called out. "Yo! Rick!"

The other deputy marshal did not answer.

"He ain't got nothin' to say just now," Red Hogan said.

Red Hogan was ready for the shooting when it started. At least, he wasn't surprised by it. When he heard Buck say there was a horse-shaped boulder in the opposite tree line, Red knew it wasn't a boulder and he knew where there was a horse there was also an ambush.

When the shooting started, Red fell back to the ground and then scurried behind Buck's saddle. He saw Rick Compton get shot.

Compton had pulled his gun and was facing the shooters when the first bullet struck him. It hit him in the chest and he reared up, snatching at his chest with his empty hand. The second rifle shot hit him in the face and spun him around. Red Hogan had seen enough men killed to know that Deputy Marshal Rick Compton was shaking hands with the Devil before his body ever hit the ground.

"Good riddance," Red murmured.

All that came in the first volley.

The second volley chewed up the ground all around Buck's saddle. The shooters were aiming for Red Hogan.

This was a surprise to him. Red didn't think they'd be aiming to kill him. Not yet, anyway.

"Fire a shot at 'em," Red called back to Buck.

"I can't see to hit nothin'," Buck said.

"I know that. But fire a shot anyway and see what they do."

"I'll not waste the shot," Deputy Buckner said.

"You got any spare rounds for that six-gun?"

"No," Buck hissed.

"Well, you ain't gonna kill enough of them with that to make a difference if you ain't got any spare rounds. Might as well shoot one off to see what they'll do. Right now they're trying to decide if we're all three dead. If you let 'em know that we ain't all dead, they'll have to try something else. If nothing else, it'll buy us a little time to figure something out. So fire off a shot and see what happens."

Buck did not like being told what to do by his own prisoner, but he also understood that Red Hogan knew a lot more about a gunfight than he ever hoped to have to learn.

Buck took aim far out toward the opposite tree line. He felt like the Colt's barrel was pointing at the sky.

He dropped the hammer and sent a shot out through the trees and across the meadow. Where it landed, Buck had no idea.

The response was rapid and brutal. The men across the meadow opened up with their rifles, and the bullets again tore through the trees, snapping branches and raining needles down all through the woods.

"Guess we know what they'll do," Red Hogan said with a chuckle.

"I'm gonna grab Compton's rifle and get down to you," Red called over. "You got the key to these shackles?"

"I've got it," Buck called back.

Red Hogan rolled a couple of times on the ground, getting closer to where Compton's rifle was sitting beside his saddle.

"All right. Here I come," Red said.

He had to clear about twenty five feet. Fifteen feet to get out of the meadow and into the trees, and another ten feet to get back to the boulder where Buck had good cover. But once he got to the tree line he'd be safe.

With Compton's rifle in hand, Buck got to his feet. He stayed down in a crouch, but as soon as he presented a target the guns across the meadow erupted in another explosion.

"Tarnation!" Red Hogan shouted, lurching forward for the trees and then falling as a bullet smashed into the back of his thigh.

Buck jumped from behind the boulder and ran up to Red, grabbing him by the shirt and dragging him back to safety.

"Got me in the leg," Red hissed through clenched teeth.

He was breathing in short, shallow bursts.

"I think they shattered the conchuckled bone," Red said.

Buck rolled him over on his side and looked at the wound.

"It's bleeding like the devil," Buck said. "I ain't sure what to do."

Red Hogan sighed heavily. The burning pain in the back of his thigh was almost more than he could stand.

"Tie my bandanna around it and that'll serve for now. Tie it right down on the hole to staunch up the bleeding."

Buck followed his instructions, and Red Hogan winced and cried out when Buck cinched the bandanna around the leg.

"Bone is busted in there," Red said. "I can feel it. I ain't gonna get far on this leg. We're gonna have to make a stand."

"They must have a score of guns over there," Buck said.

"No such thing," Red told him. "I watched when you fired off that shot and they shot back. There ain't but four of them. Maybe five if one of 'em is holding their horses."

Buck didn't want to put up an argument, but he didn't see that the odds were going to work in their favor.

"I got four shots left in my gun. That rifle

probably ain't got but twelve. We'll have a rough time making a stand with sixteen shots. Even if there is only four of them."

Red Hogan did some figuring in his head, but it was hard to consider anything with the pain coming in flashes into his brain.

"Why, that gives us four bullets a piece for 'em. I don't know about you, but if I put four bullets in a man he's gonna be dead," Red said.

"That's if every shot tells," Buck said. "Ain't likely they will."

Red pulled himself by his elbows to where he could see around the boulder.

"Get that key and undo these shackles," Red said. "We need to contemplate on how we're going to end this in a hurry. If I don't get out of here fast, I'll bleed to death."

***

"This ain't gonna go well," Red Hogan said. "I can't move my conchuckled leg at all. You a good shot, Buckner?"

"I'm a passable shot," Buck answered him. "I don't a fair amount of hunting."

Red looked him over. "I guess I'd be more confident if you weren't so skinny."

Red had his back pressed against the large boulder. Free of the shackles, he checked the chamber in Compton's Henry rifle to be sure it was loaded, and then he drew back the hammer.

"Do you reckon it's Apache?" Buck asked.

"Hell, no, it ain't Apache," Red Hogan said. "That there is the remnants of the Old Bunch, and whoever else they managed to scrounge up."

"The Old Bunch? Your gang?"

"That's right. My old ridin' partners."

"Are they here to free you?" Buck asked. He couldn't understand why Red Hogan's gang would be coming to kill him.

"Does it look like they're here to free me?" Red asked. "Them boys is here to kill me."

"But why?"

Red shook his head. "I ain't goin' into the details with you, deputy. Suffice it to know that them four men over there – or however many it is – want me dead and they won't mind killing a deputy marshal, too."

Red bit his lip. Great beads of sweat had shown up on his forehead and nose. His face was suddenly pale.

"They may have done for me already," Red confided. "This leg is bad. It could take a month, but it's like to kill me."

Buckner kept checking over the top of the boulder, and this time he saw movement. A man was stepping out of the tree line. He carried one of Colt's revolving rifles, and he was walking slow into the meadow, taking his time and searching the landscape in front of him.

"One of 'em's coming," Buckner said to Red. "Got him a Colt rifle."

Red nodded.

"That's Rusty Hale. He's carried that Colt revolving rifle since he was in the war. Think you can hit him from here?"

Buckner shook his head. "Not with this revolver," he said.

"I mean with Compton's Henry. Can you hit him with this Henry rifle?"

Buckner shrugged. "I reckon I can."

"Shoot that sonuvabitch," Red said, handing over the Henry.

Buckner leveled the Henry over the top of the boulder and lifted up the ladder sight. He took his time taking aim. Rusty Hale was looking down the barrel of his Colt rifle, and it was generally pointed toward the tree line where Red and Buck had disappeared from his sight.

Buck squeezed the trigger and the big Henry jerked against his shoulder. A puff of white smoke, and through it Deputy Buckner saw Rusty Hale jump.

Red had leaned around the boulder so that he could watch for himself.

Rusty was hit, no doubt about it, but Red did not think it was a serious wound. Rusty Hale scrambled back to the tree line, and then the rifles across the meadow opened up again, cutting hell out of the branches and pine needles overhead.

Buck and Red hugged the boulder. At least one round struck the top of the boulder and skidded across the surface of it, but that shot was blind luck rather than skilled marksmanship. But a bullet sent with blind luck could kill a man as easy as one sent with skill.

"They're all firing repeating rifles of some kind,"

Red Hogan said. "How bad do you think you hit Rusty?"

"I figure I just winged him," Buck said.

There was a moment of stillness in the wake of the shooting. And then someone from across the meadow called out.

"Red Hogan! It's Dick Hale, Red. You know what I'm here for."

Red glanced at Deputy Buckner.

"This only ends with me gettin' what I want," Dick Hale shouted. "You hear me, Red? Either you tell me what I want to know, or we'll find the woman and she'll tell me."

Buckner watched Red to see if he would respond.

"You goin' to say anything back?"

"Hell no," Red told him. "Ain't no use in sayin' nothing to him."

Buckner peered over the top of the boulder to be sure they weren't coming on again.

"What are we going to do?" Buck asked.

Red Hogan laughed at him.

"We ain't partners in this, boy," Red said. "We might be hunkered down behind the same boulder, but you and me ain't pals and we ain't partners. You're still a deputy marshal, and I'm still an outlaw."

"You're still my prisoner," Buckner bristled.

"Like hell," Red told him. "You'll never get me out of these mountains alive on this leg. And you ain't going to get me past the Old Bunch even if I was healthy and whole."

"How did they know where to find us?" Buck asked.

"It's like I told you already," Red Hogan said. "That trapper what told you about me being here, he talked. Talk gets around. It always does. And when they heard you was coming after me, they got back together figurin' on following you up here. I know it plain as day that's what happened."

"Why do they want to kill you?" Buck asked.

"That's my business."

Buck still had the Henry rifle, and he wasn't inclined to give it back. For a moment, when Red first scrambled behind the boulder, Buckner had an idea that he and Red Hogan would partner up in this thing, and when it was over Buckner figured Red would go on back to being a prisoner. If he had known Red's intentions, he'd have not undone the shackles.

"If I was you, I'd turn around and head on back up the trail the way we come," Red Hogan said. "Find a place to hide out and wait for them boys to pass. They ain't going to quit this until I'm dead. And when I'm dead, they're going to track back the way we come to go and find my cabin."

Buckner checked over the top of the rock, but he didn't see anyone coming across the meadow.

"Why will they go to find your cabin?" Buckner asked.

"Cause they think what they want is there."

"What do they want?" Buck asked.

Red Hogan shook his head. "You'd be best to get on up the trail, hide out, and let them pass. Then you can go back and report that Red Hogan is dead. Take credit for it if you want. Tell folks you killed me in a gunfight and be a hero. Rusty and Dick Hale ain't going to come out in public to argue the point."

Deputy Buckner thought about all that Red Hogan had to say. He wondered what Rick Compton would do. Maybe Compton would go back up the trail and hide out. Maybe Compton would take credit for killing Red.

But abandoning a wounded man, leaving his prisoner, and then lying about what happened – these were not things that Deputy Buckner would do. He was raised up by honest men in the hills of Arkansas, and he had a value system that would not allow him to turn his back on an injured man, turn his back on his duty, or lie about something to dress himself in glory.

That just wasn't the kind of man he was.

"I ain't going to leave you," Buckner said. "I know we ain't pals nor partners. I'm a deputy marshal and you're my prisoner, and I ain't leaving my prisoner."

Red Hogan grunted.

"If that's the case, then you stop asking me what we're going to do. Stop lookin' so scared, and get us out of this, deputy marshal."

- 5 -

Deputy Buckner immediately regretted his outburst.

Deep down, he knew he wasn't competent to get neither Red Hogan nor himself out of there alive. He would have to depend upon Red's experience, and Red seemed determined to withhold the value of his experience.

"If I can get you on that horse, you reckon you could ride?" Buckner asked.

Red scoffed a mocking laugh and shook his head.

"I can't ride. Not with a shattered leg."

"It's better than having a shot-through skull, ain't it?"

"You go get that horse and you bring it back here. I'll give it a try," Red told him.

Buckner wasn't sure how far back along the trail the gray had run. For that matter, he didn't know if it might have been shot.

"All right. Get ready. This ain't gonna be pleasant, but it's the best I can do."

"What are you thinking?" Red asked, a hint of fear in his voice.

"I'm going to heft you up onto my shoulders and tote you outta here like a bag of feed," Buckner said. "You hold onto this Henry rifle."

Buckner set the rifle on top of the boulder, a place where Red would be able to reach it once he was up on the deputy's shoulders.

Red stammered out a plea to wait, but Buckner fetched him up and then stood with Red dangling off his shoulders. Red Hogan groaned through gritted teeth. The spasms of pain shooting through his body were intense, and he thought he might vomit from the deputy's shoulder. But he took some deep breaths. Even as tears welled up in his eyes, Red got his pain under control.

"Tarnation," he breathed. "You ain't got much sympathy for a wounded man."

Buck grinned.

"I don't mean to cause you pain," Buckner said. "But settin' here behind this boulder ain't doing us no good."

Red Hogan was not a light man. But Deputy Buckner was tall and stronger than his thin frame might suggest.

The Hale brothers and whoever else they had with them couldn't possibly see down into the trees where the boulder was to know that their quarry was backtracking, and if they had any idea how bad Red's leg was shot up, they wouldn't expect the two men to make a run. Buckner hoped they would have some time before the Hale brothers discovered that they'd fled.

Buck picked his way through the trees, trying not to run Red into any low limbs. But every step seemed to jostle Red and cause fresh waves of pain. His breathing was quick and shallow as Buck made his way through the trees.

"Take it easy," Red said when Buck stumbled over an exposed root.

"I can't help it," Buck said. "I'm doing the best I can for you."

The slope through here was all downhill, and that forced Buck to take some big steps. With each one, Red groaned and cursed.

They'd not gone terribly far when Buck's thighs and calves started to burn, and he was breathing too hard to make conversation. Even so, Buck knew that each step was leading them farther away from the danger and improving their chances of getting away.

"It won't be long before they figure out that we ain't still up there," Red Hogan said after a while.

"There she is," Buck said.

Red, slumped over Buckner's shoulders, craned his neck. Through the woods he could see the dapple gray up ahead. The gray had walked a few feet off the trail into the trees and stopped in a clearing to crop some grass.

"We'll be able to move a mite faster in a minute," Buck said.

The mare paid them little mind when they got up to it, and Red bit off his exclamations of pain as Buck set him roughly on the ground.

"Sorry about that," Buck said. "Ain't an easy way to get you down."

Buck stepped over to the mare and took her by the lead. He checked her over to be sure she wasn't shot anywhere. Satisfied, he started unpacking the pannier.

"I'm just going to lay you across her back," Buck said.

He got his own Henry rifle out of its scabbard and tucked a box of bullets into his shirt. When the pannier was off the horse, Buckner got Red Hogan standing up on his one good leg.

"Look here, deputy," Red said. "I'm probably down to just a couple of hours left before I'm dead. I guess I'd rather be spared the indignity of lying across a horse's back until I'm good and dead. Get me up astride of this thing and let me ride like a man while I'm still breathing."

Buckner nodded. "If you think you can."

With no stirrups or saddle, it was a chore, but Buck managed to heave and push until Red Hogan was astride the horse, and the mare was patient with them.

"I won't be able to stand a gallop," Red said.

"I reckon not," Buck told him.

With Red astride the horse, Buck had his first good look at the leg since he'd put the bandanna on it, and what he saw was not encouraging. The back of Red's trousers were thick with blood. Red was bleeding out. The wound was almost surely mortal.

Red toted Compton's Henry and Buckner carried his own. Buck led the horse out to the trail, and they were again overlooking the gorge where the Pecos River ran down below them.

The horse picked its way cautiously back down the trail, littered with loose rocks and pine roots. Buck let the horse go first and he followed, keeping a watch on their back trail.

It did not take much imagination to see what was happening back at the meadow – whether it had already happened or would happen soon. One of them, maybe Rusty Hale again, or maybe one of the others, would take a few cautious steps out of the tree line and into the meadow. They'd be nervous because Buck had winged Rusty from across the meadow the first time they tried it. They'd take a few tentative steps, growing in confidence as they moved. Then, at some point, they'd crouch down, nervous that they were getting into better killing range. They'd get near to where Compton's body was lying. Then they'd break the tree line and see the boulder. They'd see no one was there. They'd signal to the others, and that's when the Old Bunch would be back on the trail.

Buck did not know if it would take them ten minutes or an hour before they braved it. He just knew he wanted to put as much distance between him and the others as he could.

The trail continued to drop until at last it began to level out and once again they were down in the valley and moving along beside the Pecos.

"They've figured out we ain't still up there by now," Red said, and the sound of his voice startled Buck. The man's words came out soft and weak. He was slumped on the back of the horse, and Deputy Buckner didn't think he'd ever seen a man look so pale and still be alive.

"We've got to do something for you," Buck said, but he did not know what to do. He'd never treated a man with a gunshot wound before.

Up ahead the trail broke into a clearing.

Buck remembered this place from earlier in the day when they'd come through here in the opposite direction. The trees thinned out and the grass grew high with large boulders spread all around. They probably weren't much more than a couple of miles now from the place where they'd camped the night before.

If the Old Bunch were close behind, this would prove to be a dangerous place. If they came down off the ridge now, they'd have a clear shot at Buck and Red as they crossed the open area. What worried Buck the most was that the Old Bunch would be able to move faster. They'd be mounted, riding with saddles. They'd easily catch up.

Even as the thought went through his mind, Buckner watched Red Hogan lean heavily. Buck started forward with his hand outstretched, but he was too late to prevent Red from sliding out of the saddle and landing heavily on the ground.

When he fell, he spooked the horse and it started at a run, leaving Red and Buckner behind.

***

Red Hogan spluttered.

"I'm done for," he said.

"Not yet," Buckner told him. The deputy took hold of the front of Red's shirt and hefted him up, holding him as Red stood on his one good leg. The other leg just sort of dangled to the ground, worthless.

"Yeah I am, boy," Red said.

"As long as you're breathing, I'm going to get you out of here," Buckner said.

"It ain't no use," Red Hogan said, and his breathing was labored.

A large boulder nearby was just about the right height to lean Red against it, and Buckner started to make his way to it, helping Red has he hobbled along on one leg.

They were nearly there when the crack of a rifle broke the air and Buckner heard the bullet whistle past them.

He glanced down the backtrail, and there at the edge of the clearing he saw five riders. Three of them had rifles up and ready, and even as Buckner watched, two of them let loose a cloud of smoke followed by the loud crack.

Deputy Buckner felt the punch of the bullet as it hit Red Hogan in the back of his hip. Immediately, Red started to slide to the ground, and Buckner, his arms wrapped around the man, struggled to keep Red upright.

Buck made two or three bounding jerks, dragging Red, and the two men collapsed behind the big boulder.

Red Hogan was groaning now, taking in short breaths that stopped suddenly. He coughed and spluttered blood.

On the ground, Buck rolled Hogan over onto his stomach and looked at the fresh wound. They'd shot him just below the belt and just right of his spine.

More bullets came down range now, smashing into the rock where they were hiding.

Buck had dropped his Henry rifle, and Red Hogan had dropped Compton's rifle, so that their only weapon was Buck's Colt Army. The two rifles were five yards away and the Old Bunch were fifty yards away.

Buck peered over the large rock and saw that the other men were dismounting and spreading out.

"You still think I'm going to make it out of here?" Red Hogan asked.

Buck looked at him. Red had rolled himself onto his back and was propped up on an elbow.

"I ain't sure either of us will make it out," Buck admitted.

"Probably not," Hogan said. "Can you get to them rifles?"

"If they don't shoot me I can."

"Send a couple of balls down range at them with your revolver," Hogan said. "Make 'em duck their heads. Then make a dash for them rifles. I'm going to get you out of here, Buckner, but you're going to have to make me a promise."

Buck slid his Colt from his holster and glanced over the top of the boulder. The Old Bunch weren't advancing. They were holding their positions. They'd spread out so that there were probably ten feet between each man. One man was holding the horses back a ways, the other four were at the edge of the clearing. The four had their rifles up, and they all seemed to be pointed directly at Buck. He dipped his head back down.

"They're going to try to get around you to the sides. Flank you. Rusty and Dick Hale was both in the war, and they still think in terms of tactics. You understand?"

Buck nodded.

"You've got to keep them from flanking you," Red said. "Only way to do that is to scare them into holding their ground where they are. Take a couple of shots and then get them rifles. Both of them."

Red's breathing was labored, and it was a chore for him to talk. But he had a determination now that Buck hadn't seen in him before. He was fighting through the pain to see this through.

Buck took a breath to drum up his courage, and then he popped up over the top of the rock.

He dropped the hammer on the Colt, and his first shot was better than he'd intended. It came so near to Rusty Hale and one of the others that both men dropped to the ground.

Buck had already taken two big strides out toward the guns when he cocked back the hammer on the Colt for another shot. Dick Hale and one of the others both opened fire and chewed chunks out of the boulder where Red Hogan was still hiding.

Buck pointed the Colt roughly in the direction of Dick Hale and the other man and let loose another shot while he was still on the run.

Then he holstered the Colt and snatched up both rifles. He turned and made a diving leap and hit the ground beside Red.

"Get up and give 'em hell," Red said.

Buck got to his knees, still crouched in safety behind the boulder, and he raised the Henry to his shoulder. He came around the edge of it this time, and he had a clear view down field of one of the four men. It was the one who was trying to come around to the right with Rusty Hale.

Deputy Buckner held the rifle steady, peered down the sight. He let out a slow breath and squeezed the trigger, just the way his grandfather taught him to do hunting whitetails back in Arkansas.

The bullet smashed into the man's chest and staggered him. He dropped his own rifle and stumbled, first forward and then back, and then he dropped to the ground.

That was the first man Buckner had ever killed.

Like killing a deer or an elk, Buckner didn't feel any great sense of celebration or relief. He felt the burden of a life passing.

But an elk or deer would feed him, sustain him. Killing a deer or an elk would keep Buck alive. The same was true with shooting this outlaw. Killing that man would keep Buck alive.

There was shouting down range as the Old Bunch gang realized one of their own had been killed.

"You get him?" Red asked.

"I got him," Buckner said.

"Get another," Red told him.

Buckner scooted himself around the boulder and tried to find his next target. But the Old Bunch had all gone to ground, seeking cover behind clumps of grass or bushes. All Buckner had were legs or elbows or tops of heads to try to shoot, and the angle for making the shot was all wrong.

Even so, he dropped the lever on the Henry rifle

and sent another round down range. He followed that up fast with another. And then another.

"Keep peppering them conchuckled sonsabitches," Red said, and there was the tiniest note of excitement in his voice.

Buckner let loose with another round of shots. He'd send one at one target and then move quickly to another. By himself, he was successfully forcing the three surviving men in the Old Bunch to keep their heads down.

The fourth living member of the outlaw gang, the one holding the horses, had moved farther back and out of sight.

But the three who were trying to flank him were now pinned down by just one man.

When the hammer on Buckner's Henry fell on an empty chamber, Red pushed the other rifle to him.

"Keep 'em going!" Red Hogan said, and there was a grin on his ghostly pale face. The excitement of a fight had given Red a little bit of life back. "Toss me them shells and I'll reload you."

Buckner slowed his rate of fire now. He picked his target and squeezed the trigger. The bullet kicked up sand very near to Rusty Hale's head.

But when Buckner tried to drop the lever to chamber another round the gun was jammed.

The open ejection top of the Henry always made it susceptible to dirt that could jam the gun. Buckner blew into the open top and banged the gun against the boulder, and finally he was able to get the next round to load.

But the time it took to get the gun operating again had given the Old Bunch an opportunity to regroup.

Rather than charge forward, the men drew back, gathering behind their own boulder.

Buck's ears were ringing from so many successive shots. He felt an elation that he'd never experienced before, and he wondered if this was bloodlust. He'd heard about it from old veterans, about soldiers in the thick of battle who would get their dander up in the fight. Most of what he'd heard were cautionary tales – men would get so caught up in the battle that they'd do some damned fool thing like rise up and make a solitary charge.

Buck understood that. His heart was racing. His blood was pumping. He didn't feel any fear at the moment. He felt invincible, like he wanted to jump up on top of the boulder he was hiding behind and go at these men who were threatening to kill him.

But he kept cool.

"Trade me rifles. I'll reload. Hold your fire now," Red told him. "Don't shoot unless they give you a good target."

Buck took the loaded rifle and nodded.

"Now you listen to me," Red Hogan said. "I'm as good as dead right here. I won't live another hour. I'm shot all to hell and Satan is waitin'. But I'll get you out of this alive if you'll promise me something."

Deputy Buckner narrowed his eyes. Young as he was, he knew some things about honor and right and wrong. And he knew that if a man made a promise to another man, especially a dying man, it wasn't a promise that could be made lightly. And feeling the way he did,

Buckner didn't know that he needed Red Hogan's help in getting out of this fix. Right now, Deputy Buckner was pretty certain he could save himself.

But Red Hogan was dying, and he was making a request, and Buckner wasn't the sort of man who could ignore that.

"Promise you what?" Buck asked.

- 6 -

Red Hogan straightened himself up some.

Every movement made him wretch. He could feel the shattered bone shifting inside his leg. He could feel the blood leaking out of his body. The bullet in his hip felt like it was scraping against his bone every time he shifted. But riding along on that horse, knowing that the end was coming, Red Hogan had one thought in mind. Somewhere behind him, a woman was carrying his child. And that child was Red Hogan's only chance of redemption in this life. If he was going to leave behind him anything worthwhile or good, it was going to have to come from that child. And now, like never before, as death hung over him like a cloud, Red Hogan had a yearning to leave behind him something worthwhile.

"My pregnant woman," Red said. "Teresa."

"What about her?" Buck asked.

"Dick and Rusty Hale are going for her. If it was just a matter of surviving the winter alone at that cabin, I'm confident she can do it. Even birthing the baby. She'd be all right. She's as strong as an ox. Tougher than any woman you'll ever find. You understand what I mean, Buckner?"

Buck nodded. He looked over the boulder to be sure the Old Bunch were still down behind their own boulder. Buck raised up the Henry and fired a shot that skidded across the top of the big rock down range.

"Just giving them something to think about so they don't come charging," Buck said.

"Listen to me. I ain't got long."

Buck nodded.

"Teresa would be fine if it was just a matter of getting by. She could make it on her own for a year or two in that cabin if she had to. But Dick and Rusty are going to go for her. Stealing the horses. I've been thinking on it, and I reckon they thought we'd turn around if the horses was stole. They figured we'd go back to the cabin, and they thought they could follow us there. But we didn't turn around, so now they're going to kill me. And they're going to kill you. And then they're going to trail our tracks back up to the cabin. And when they get there, they're going to kill Teresa."

"But why?" Buck asked.

Red coughed, and blood splattered across his lips.

"Because when they get to the cabin, they ain't gonna find what they're looking for. Now maybe they'll beat Teresa until she tells them. Or maybe they'll beat her and she never says. But one way or another, whether she tells them or not, they'll kill her. Because that's who they are."

"What are they looking for?" Buck asked.

"When the gang broke up, after them deputies came for us, I made off with all the loot."

At the memory of it, Red grinned, and a sparkle came into his eyes. He laughed a little, and that turned into a bloody cough.

"It's quite a sum. Silver coins, greenbacks, a little bit of gold. I reckon all told, it's about forty thousand dollars."

Buckner drew back in surprise.

"That much?"

Red laughed, and the laugh turned into another spluttering cough. This one was worse than the others, and while he coughed, Buckner fired off another round at the distant boulder.

When the fit came to an end, Red's eyes had lost their sparkle.

"I didn't do no good in my life, but I was good at what I did."

Red's breathing became more labored. His eyelids drooped.

"We got to move fast," he said. "I'm all give out."

Red's eyes searched Deputy Buckner's face.

"You're an honest man. I can see that in you. Make the promise."

"Promise what?" Buck asked.

"Did you hear what she said to me back at the cabin? She said she never loved me and she would be certain my child didn't turn out like me. Those words cut deep, Buckner. And I've been thinking hard on it."

"Promise what?"

"Promise you'll go back and get Teresa out. Get her and my baby. Get them out of here. She knows where the loot is buried. They's some of it back at the cabin, but not enough to trifle with. She knows where the whole thing is buried. I intended to go and get it, maybe in a year or two when things had calmed down and folks wasn't looking so hard for me. But if you go and get her now, you can split the loot with her. Half to her and half to you. It's money enough for her to raise my child into something decent, something better than I ever was. And it's money enough to make it worth your while to keep your promise."

"I don't want stolen loot," Deputy Buckner said.

"Then turn in your half. I don't care. Half to her and half to you. And if you promise, I'll get you out of this alive."

Buckner shook his head.

"I ain't making no deal with the Devil," Buckner said.

"Then you'll shake hands with the sonuvabitch in a minute," Red spat. "You think them boys in my old outfit ain't gonna kill you directly? Just cause you shot one don't mean you've won a damn thing. Make the promise to get Teresa out before they get to her, and I'll save your neck."

Red Hogan was struggling to even speak now.

"My old outfit. The Old Bunch. They'll be up after Teresa as soon as they've done for us. You saw her. Pregnant like she is. A woman alone. She won't stand a chance. And God alone knows what they'll do to her. They'll know I told her where to find the loot. And they'll do whatever it takes to make her tell them. Whatever it takes."

It did not make a difference if it was intentional or happenstance, but Red Hogan had now lit on the fuse that would spark a reaction from Deputy Buckner.

Buckner wasn't interested in the value of the loot. He couldn't be bribed because he was still young enough that he believed in a code of honor that made him reject the notion of a bribe.

And Buckner couldn't be scared into it. Like all young men, death was an abstract notion to him, nothing he contemplated in terms of what it might mean to him personally. He was young enough to still wonder if he might never die.

But a woman alone and defenseless against a gang of outlaws – that was something that Deputy Buckner could not abide.

Buckner nodded.

"I'll get her out," he said.

Red Hogan actually breathed a clean breath, a satisfied sigh.

He reached up and put a hand on Buckner's shirt front and pulled the young deputy closer to him.

"Listen to what I say to you now. Leave one of them rifles with me. I'll lay down some covering fire for you to make tracks back down this trail. Find that damn gray mare. Ride her to where I left my saddle, where we made camp. Saddle her up so you can ride her good and fast, and get up to Teresa before nightfall. I'll do what I can to hold them off as long as I can. But you can't count on that bein' long."

Buck nodded.

"They'll either get me or I'll pass on, and it'll happen soon, either way."

Red Hogan struggled to get enough strength together to keep talking.

"When you get to the cabin, start out right away. Don't wait for light. They'll stop come nightfall, but that's your chance to put distance betwixt you. Cut out through the mountains to the east. There's a pass northeast of my cabin. Teresa might be able to find it. Through that pass there's valleys that all link up. Once your east of the mountains, drop south and you'll walk right into the plaza in Las Vegas. That's where the loot is buried, out in Las Vegas. Teresa knows where. Tell her to get that money and head east. Tell her to take her half and go to St. Louis or Chicago or Baltimore. She'll have money enough to take care of herself and the child, and if she goes somewhere back east then Dick and Rusty will leave her alone. They won't bother her if she goes east."

Red coughed up some more blood, and he winced as the coughing sent pain all through his back and leg.

"You understand all that? East. Just keep going east."

"I understand," Buckner said.

"Tell her to raise that baby right."

"I will," Buck said.

"Swear it to me. Make the promise."

"I promise," Deputy Buckner said. "I promise I'll get Teresa out of the mountains. I promise I won't let them men get to her. And I promise I'll tell her that you want her to do right by your baby."

"That's a debt, Buck," Red said. "That promise is a debt you owe me. Now, prop me up on top of this boulder with that rifle. And then get the hell out of here."

Buck wrenched Red up off the ground, and the pain was such that Red Hogan screamed when Buck set him down on the boulder.

Red was lying there, unable to move himself from the waist down.

"Go boulder to boulder," Red said. "Keep running when you're out in the open. I'll hold 'em off as long as I can."

Buckner did not wait. He crouched low and started to make a run.

As soon as he was out in the open he heard shots from behind. The Old Bunch were trying to get him.

Two shots fired right away. Then a third, and then a fourth. The sand at his feet kicked up. A bullet smashed into the side of a big rock as Buck ran past it.

Then Red Hogan fired a return shot.

A fifth shot came from the Old Bunch, and Red shot again.

Buck scrambled down behind a big boulder. A bullet ricocheted off the boulder just as Buck got down behind it.

Red Hogan fired another shot, and then two rifle cracks in quick succession, and Red let out a squeal.

Buck looked back and saw that Red had been shot again, this time in his arm. But he was working the lever on the Henry with one hand, sliding the gun around on the big boulder to try to aim it.

Buck stood up and sprinted as fast as he could back down the trail. He was nearly to the edge of the clearing now, and the shots were coming fast behind him.

He could tell from the sound of the shooting that Red was still managing to get off a shot every few seconds.

Now Buckner was against surrounded by trees. His breath was hard to catch in his chest, but he kept running. The Pecos River ran along beside him, and he scanned the riverbank ahead for any sight of the dapple gray. Still behind him he heard an occasional shot, and Buck was perplexed that Red Hogan was still putting up a fight.

The trail rounded a bend, following the course of the river, and there was the dapple gray, standing at the bank drinking.

She held still as Buck took up her lead.

He leaned against the horse for a moment, trying to catch his breath. And then he stepped up on a big rock and swung his leg over the horse.

"Let's go girl," Buck said.

In the distance behind him, Buckner no longer heard gunshots.

- 7 -

Deputy Buckner almost rode past the campsite. He was driving the mare as hard as she could go. It was the ring of rocks where Compton had built the fire that caught his eye, and he pulled in the reins on the gray and turned her toward the place where Red had left his saddle.

Buck's hands were shaking as he swung the saddle over the horse's back and began to cinch it tight, and he realized he was afraid.

He did not know, but he hoped that his fear was for the pregnant woman back at the cabin. He worried, though, that his fear was for himself.

It was agonizing watching Red Hogan die. Compton went fast, but Red died slow, in a lot of pain, and with three bullet holes in him the last time Buck saw him. Buck was scared of being shot, scared of having his bones shatter inside him, scared of bleeding out.

"Now we just got to find that deer path," Buck said to the horse.

They'd ridden quite a ways beside the Pecos before camping the night before, but Buck had paid little attention.

Still, as he rode now he caught sight of landmarks. Rocks or oddly shaped trees that he recognized.

The ride back, too, always seemed shorter than the ride there. As landmarks came along they brought back to memory the trail ahead, and Buck found himself remembering more of the trail than he realized he would.

And when he caught sight of a tall bluff on the opposite bank at the bend of the river, he knew he was close to the path that led up to Red Hogan's cabin. The horse was at nothing more than a trot now, and Buck pulled the reins and then dismounted.

He led the horse on foot, knowing he was giving the Old Bunch space to catch him. But missing the path would be worse than allowing the men behind him to close the gap.

And then he saw it. Just the tiniest gap in the trees. It looked like a tiny opening to a cave, an almost imperceptible gap in the trees and branches. But this was it, an old deer path leading up the slope.

Buck stood for a moment, holding the horse's lead. He wondered if he had time for a ruse. He tried to think how long Red Hogan must have held off his old gang and wondered if he had time to lead the horse past the trail.

But already the sun was behind the western ridges and everything in the Pecos valley was becoming shadows. Buck abandoned those thoughts and turned the horse into the trees. There he climbed back into the saddle and rode the horse up the slope, following the deer path.

Several times he saw boulders or tall pines or other natural signs that told him he was on the right path.

An hour, maybe, and he'd be with Teresa at Hogan's cabin. But it would be dark by then, or nearly so. Buck wondered if they would have light enough to escape the cabin, or if they would be forced to wait until morning.

As he rode into a stand of aspen trees, Buck knew he was nearly there. These were just about the only aspens he'd seen. The stand of aspens is where Buck dropped the blanket with the guns rolled up in it. As he passed the spot he saw that Teresa had come for them.

And then he broke into the meadow, and in the gloaming he could make out the cabin up ahead and the corral. He saw smoke from the chimney, but Red was right that the smoke did not linger here. Buck still did not smell it, even this close to the cabin.

As he rode through the meadow and past the corral, the cabin door opened and Teresa Hogan stood there with the shotgun.

Buck rode right up to the front of the cabin and swung himself out of the saddle.

"I expected Red," Teresa said. "I thought he would have killed you and the other deputy by now."

Buck shrugged.

"No, ma'am. That didn't happen."

"Why are you here, deputy?"

"Ma'am, we was ambushed. Deputy Compton was killed. And Red was shot up pretty bad."

Teresa drew a quick breath, almost like she'd been punched.

Buck wasn't sure how she would respond, learning that her husband was dead. But she didn't cry or wail or show any emotion at all, really. Just that quick breath.

"But you got away?" Teresa said.

"Yes, ma'am."

"And you came back here."

"Yes, ma'am."

"Why, Deputy Buckner? Why would you come back here? Did you return so that you could lead the Apache here?"

"It wasn't Apache that ambushed us," Buck said. "It was your husband's old gang. Or what's left of it. Dick and Rusty Hale."

Teresa looked past Buck at the clearing.

"So you've brought the Old Bunch here?"

"Red seemed to think they were coming anyway," Buck said. "He made me promise to come back and get you out."

Teresa looked past him again, watching the far side of the meadow for any sign of riders. Buck turned around for a look, too, but it was too dark to see much of anything among the trees now.

"I relieve you of your promise," Teresa said. "I won't leave here."

"Ma'am, Red seemed to think those men were coming here with the intention of killing you," Buck said. "From what I've seen, Red was probably right."

Teresa narrowed her eyes at him, and Buck could not help but notice how beautiful she was in the dim light coming down from the sky and the orange glow cast from the fire inside the cabin.

"You say that, deputy, as if death would be such a terrible thing."

Buck nodded at her. "Ma'am, I understand. But you're carrying a baby. If you can't think of yourself, you should think of the baby."

"What life can I offer a child in this cabin?" Teresa asked. "I have no money. Every day in these mountains you work yourself half to death just to have enough food so that an empty belly does not keep you from falling asleep. And you sleep only to have enough rest to get up and do it all again."

"What about the loot?" Buck asked.

"The loot?" Teresa said.

"Red Hogan said you know where it's at."

Teresa laughed a mocking laugh.

"If I knew where Red Hogan buried his treasure, I would not have been here with him for these last two years. I can promise you that."

Buck shook his head. "He said you knew. He said it was buried in Las Vegas, and you knew where."

Suddenly a flash of recognition crossed Teresa's face.

"Before you took him," she said. "He whispered to me. He said to find the grave for Red Chavez in the churchyard of the red stone church."

"Do you know the church?" Buck asked.

"I do know the church. Our Lady of Sorrows," Teresa said.

"That must be where it's buried. In Red Chavez's grave."

"It is his joke," Teresa said. "There is no Red Chavez. Chavez is my maiden name. It's his name and my name. He just buried his money under a stone with our names."

The recognition of where to find the money seemed to have shaken Teresa from her dour mood.

"So let me take you out of here," Buck said.

Teresa nodded.

"Yes, Deputy Buckner. In the morning we will go."

"Not in the morning," Buck said. "We must leave now. We'll saddle a couple of fresh horses and go."

Teresa laughed.

"Deputy Buckner. Look at me. I am pregnant. I cannot ride a horse."

"Then how?" Buck asked.

"We can't walk out of these mountains," he said.

Teresa looked helplessly at him.

"There is no other way."

***

"Come in, Deputy Buckner," Teresa said, and she reached out and took Buck by the wrist and pulled him into the cabin. She shut the door behind him.

"It is getting cold," she said, and Teresa walked to a chair where there was a colorful blanket that she wrapped around herself.

"The pass through the mountains will put us on the eastern slope," she said. "There is a little village in the valley, Rociada. We will go through the village and follow the trail to Las Vegas. This is the way Red and I first came into the mountains. Once we are through the pass there are valleys that will take us east. It is not so bad a journey. No more than three days."

Buck shook his head. "You don't understand. I ain't worried about walking, but they'll catch us. Even if we leave right now, if we're walking then they'll catch us for certain."

Teresa sat down in a chair, and Buck also sat.

"You must be hungry," she said. "I have a stew on the fire. Let me get some for you."

"Miss Teresa," Buck said. "We're in real danger. These are dangerous men, and they're determined."

Teresa nodded as she went to the fire with a bowl. She ladled stew into the bowl and handed it to Buck.

"I do understand," she said. "But I cannot ride a horse. We can only do what we can do, Deputy Buckner. This evening we will prepare for our journey. In the morning, at first light, we will start to make our way. And whatever comes, we will deal with it then."

Buck found her attitude strangely calming. It was the same, cool attitude that she adopted when she realized that she was going to be left alone at the mountain cabin. It was an inner strength, and Buck marveled at it.

He took a couple of spoonfuls of the stew.

"How is it you're so young and so calm?" Buck asked.

Teresa smiled at him. She had a very pretty smile.

"Life is very hard, Deputy Buckner. A person can only fret over it so much."

Buck searched her face and wondered how hard her life had been. For a woman so young, she had very sad looking eyes, and Buck saw that even when she smiled she looked sad.

"I need to tend to the horse," Buck said.

He set down the stew and went outside. He took the saddle off the gray and turned her out in the corral.

He spent several unnecessary minutes outside listening in the darkness, but he heard nothing.

When he went back inside, Teresa was packing saddlebags with salted meat and biscuits. She nodded to him.

"Finish your stew, Deputy Buckner," Teresa said. "You will need your strength."

Buck sat down at the table and continued to eat.

"My parents died when I was very young," Teresa said. "My father was killed in an accident, and a month later my mother died giving birth to my sibling. If it was a boy or girl, I do not know. Orphaned. I was taken in by a cousin to my mother and her husband. When I was young, my mother's cousin beat me and forced me to work for her. And when I was older, but still too young, her husband had his way with me. I ran away from them the moment I was able, and the only way I could find to take care of myself was laying with men for money.

Buck listened without comment.

"When Red Hogan came along with a promise of something different, I took that chance. Everything is always a chance. And for the past several months, my life with Red was more tolerable than anything I can remember. But Red was lazy and did not want to live this life. He hungered to return to the outlaw trails with his friends. He always missed riding into villages and feeling like a king."

Teresa looked at him.

"And now Red is gone and you are here. And I can take a chance to run with you or I can take a chance to stay here. You are young, and nice to look at, and you call me 'ma'am' and you are polite. I cannot remember the last man I met who was so polite. So I will take a chance with you, Deputy Buckner."

Buck found it was hard to swallow the stew.

Teresa laughed.

"You look at me like you do not know if you should kiss me or run from me."

Buck took a deep breath.

"Yes, ma'am," he said. "I reckon that is how I'm looking at you."

"So which will it be, Deputy Buckner?"

Buck nodded slightly.

"I reckon neither," he said.

Teresa's smiled faded.

"I think, deputy, you may be the first man to ever look at me like that and not decide to do one or the other. For most men, the decision came to whether or not they had the silver coins to afford the kiss. But I would kiss you for free."

"It's best if we just get together what we can tonight so that we can be gone by first light. Has Red got a pannier?"

"Over there," Teresa said with a nod.

"Do you have a saddle?"

"I do, but I cannot ride," Teresa said.

"I know that," Buck said. "But we'll saddle two horses and take a pack horse. If it comes to it, you'll ride and take your chances. But the promise I made to Red Hogan was that I'd get you and your baby out of here. And that's what I intend to do."

- 8 -

Deputy Buckner struggled in the dark to bring in the three horses from the corral. Even with a lantern lit, it was too dark to see much of anything, and the horses did not know him.

He did manage to wrangle the dapple gray mare he'd been riding. He appreciated the horse. Despite the shooting, it had never run too far, and the gray had been a calm and obedient horse. She gave him speed when he needed it, and she seemed to have good endurance.

The others were black and a dark bay, and both looked like good saddle horses.

He saddled two of the horses and put the pannier on the third. There was not much to take. Some blankets, some food, a spare rifle and the scattergun and one of Red Hogan's cap and ball pistols. He found a couple of canteens that he filled.

As he worked, getting the horses and the provisions ready for the journey, Buck considered how close the Old Bunch might be.

They were probably never very far behind him the previous afternoon. The shooting with Red Hogan was over while Buck was still in earshot.

Tracking him, they would have moved slower than he was going. But probably not much slower because, after all, they were tracking him on an easily seen trail.

The only opportunity to have caused them confusion was when he left the trail along the Pecos for the deer path up the slope to the cabin.

They could not have followed that path in the dark.

But if they'd reached the deer path, they wouldn't need more than an hour of daylight to arrive at the cabin. If they were somewhere along that deer path when night fell and they had to stop, they could be at the cabin even sooner.

And when he looked up, the sky was already blue in the east.

Teresa insisted on having a fire in the fireplace through the night. She said she was too cold without it, and Buck conceded that the mountain night was chilly.

"We'll have to make tracks soon," Buck said, walking back into the cabin. "They could be here any time after daylight."

Teresa had the same blanket from the night before wrapped over her shoulders.

"We should eat first," she said. "Have some stew."

Buck agreed, though he did not have much appetite. But he knew Teresa needed to eat.

"Can you find the pass?" Buck asked.

"I can. Red and I used to go to it frequently so that we could find our way if we had to. He always believed if danger came it would come from the Pecos trail. But we also walked down to the Pecos frequently so that we could find our way there. For all his confidence, Red was always very nervous. Especially when we first came into the mountains together. Our days were spent building the cabin, making the garden, chopping wood for the winter. Our evenings were spent preparing to flee if we had to."

Buck nodded. He understood why.

"Did you know he'd stolen money from his gang?"

Teresa smiled her sad smile.

"Not at first. I think Red believed that if he had told me about the money when we first came here I would have tried to take it from him and leave. And I might have."

"Did you love him?" Buck asked.

Teresa laughed.

"Oh, Deputy Buckner, whoever loves anyone? People stay together because it's easier for two than one. Nobody loves."

Buck shrugged.

"I don't think that's true," Buck said.

Teresa's laugh was mocking, and she spoke in a tone that a person might use with a child.

"Does a man love a woman? Or does he just want someone to lay with at night, and someone to make his supper? Does a woman love a man? Or does she just need someone to give her shelter and someone to butcher a cow? Love is a word that has no value. There is no emotion that goes with that word, Deputy Buckner. Oh, maybe a love a mother feels for a child. But most children born into this world are a burden and a curse."

Buck pursed his lips.

"That's a lonely way of looking at life," he said.

Teresa shrugged.

"Did I love Red Hogan? My only thought when you took him away was that my safety was leaving. The man who provided for me and would see me through my pregnancy was being taken from me. I did not care that he was going to a rope, and I did not shed a tear when you came back here and told me he was dead. And yet, this is the man who gave me the easiest time of my life. He never beat me, and he made sure I was warm and fed. Is that the same thing as love?"

Buck scraped his bowl with his spoon and took a last bite.

"We should go," he said.

Teresa looked around the cabin one last time.

"I will miss this place."

The Henry rifle was leaning against the door frame, and Buck picked it up as he pushed open the door.

Morning had broken, gray with a misty fog hanging low in the trees.

Even with the fog, Buck's eyes caught the movement out in the meadow beyond the corral.

"Dangit," Buck exclaimed, and he stopped in the door frame.

Four riders far out across the meadow. They'd just come up off the deer path trail. The fourth rider trailed three horses. Two of them were the stolen horses Rick Compton and Red Hogan had ridden. The other horse, Buck guessed, must have belonged to the outlaw Buck shot and killed.

He was disappointed that Red hadn't injured any of the others so bad that they had to be left behind.

"What is wrong?" Teresa asked. She'd been following him out of the cabin, and Buck was filling the doorway so that she could not see.

"Riders," Buck said. "Across the meadow. That's them."

"What can we do?" Teresa asked.

Buck did not answer. As he watched, the riders reined in and dismounted.

Again, the last man held the horses, even walking them back a ways toward the edge of the meadow.

The other three began a cautious approach. The stepped well wide of each other so as to keep from being picked off easily.

They were outside of easy rifle shot.

Buck's stomach twisted into knots as he tried to decide what was best to do.

Staying in cabin seemed like the poorest option. They could surround them and burn them out.

But running also seemed a poor option. On the trail, they would be exposed. And on foot instead of horseback, Buck and Teresa could never hope to get away.

Buck looked around the cabin.

Red Hogan took the time to cut windows in all

four walls when he built the cabin. Most mountain folks would have gone without a window. But Red built an outlaw cabin, one that could be defended and, importantly, one that could provide an escape.

"Can you shimmy out that back window?" Buck asked.

"I can," Teresa said. "I am pregnant, but not helpless."

"Get out the window and wait for me at the back of the cabin."

Buck took a deep breath to steady himself, and then he pushed open the door, stepped wide around the corral and he fired off two quick shots from the Henry rifle.

The three approaching men all dropped to the ground. Buck was pleased to see his shots land close enough to make the men nervous. He sent another shot down the way and then hurried over to where the three horses were tied.

All he could do was point the horses in the right direction and hope. He untied the horses and directed them to the edge of the cabin. Then he gave the gray a slap on the hind quarter, and the mare took off running. The other two followed.

Quickly, Buck sent another couple of shots down range at the three men in the Old Bunch. As he did, the Old Bunch returned fire and bullets smashed into the cabin walls near him.

Buck hurried back inside the cabin, pulling the door closed.

Teresa was already climbing through the back

window.

"Just wait for me right there," Buck said to her.

He pushed the door open again and saw what he expected. The three outlaws were crouched and running toward opposite sides of the meadow. They were going to try to come around the flanks of the cabin.

Buck fired first in one direction and then in the other. The men dropped to the ground, and then returned fire. Buck stepped back inside and pulled the door closed.

He wasn't going to have much time.

The cabin backed up to the tree line. Buck's intention was to make the Old Bunch think he was still inside the cabin and then sneak away out the back window and through the woods. At best, it might give them a ten minute head start. He hoped that somewhere along the trail they might catch the horses he'd just turned loose.

The ruse would only work, though, if Buck could convince them he was still in the cabin.

He pushed the door open again and fired the Henry rifle.

It was a lucky shot, and Buck was certain he hit the man trying to come around the left side. They were all still far out in the meadow, and Buck couldn't be certain, but he saw the man fall.

He fired off another shot to try to keep them down, and then Buck pulled the door to.

He heard the men shouting at each other in the meadow, and he cracked the door. He couldn't make out what they were saying, but he was convinced that he'd hit the man on the left and that man was calling for help.

Now was the time.

Buck grabbed a chair and set it by the door. He took one of Red's rifles and cracked the door open. He had to tie it to keep it from falling open the whole way. Then Buck set the rifle stock down on the back of the chair, laying the barrel on the rope that he'd tied from the handle to a peg on the wall.

The gun sat lopsided, but he hoped from a distance it would look like a man was in the doorway holding a rifle.

Now Buck scrambled out the back window.

"That ain't gonna fool them for long," Buck said to Teresa.

He took her by the arm, and they hurried into the woods, using the cabin to shelter them from view.

They went quickly for thirty-five or forty yards, pushing through undergrowth and getting deep enough that in the dim morning light, with the fog, Buck was confident the men across the meadow would not see them.

"Did you see which way the horses went?" Buck asked.

"That way," Teresa pointed. "There is a trail there that leads to the pass, and the horses made for that trail."

Buck nodded and grinned at her.

"That's lucky for us," he said. "Let's keep moving. We'll go deeper into the woods and then cut out toward that trail. Hopefully we can find the horses on our way."

***

There was a volley of shooting in the distance behind them, and Buck figured that was the Old Bunch making a dash toward the cabin. They'd fire off a couple of rounds each and then charge the place. They'd probably been slowly, cautiously making their way to it this whole time.

"Keep your eyes open for them horses," Buck said.

Teresa was breathing hard. She was a strong woman, but the pregnancy made hiking through the woods difficult for her.

"They will catch up to us," she said, the words coming out in heavy breaths.

"I know," Buck said.

He took her by the elbow as she stepped over a fallen tree.

"We need to get up to the trail, see if we can't find the horses," Buck said.

"It is just over there," Teresa said, pointing. "Do you see the open area there?"

Buck nodded, but she was not looking at him.

"I see it," he said.

"That is where the trail is."

"How easy is it to find from the cabin?" Buck asked.

"Not hard," Teresa said. "The meadow curls back a ways and the trail begins at the end of the meadow. The meadow is almost like a funnel the way it narrows down to the trail."

"That ain't good news," Buck said. "But it means the horses almost surely went for the trail."

They hurried along a little farther, edging closer to the trail the whole way. They'd gone maybe a mile or a mile and a half when they saw all three horses standing in a clearing.

"Oh, thank God!" Teresa said.

Buck hurried up to the horses. None of them tried to bolt. He patted them as he took their leads. Teresa caught up to him and he gave the lead of one horse to her.

"Even if we just go at a walk, any distance that you think you can ride is better than walking," Buck said.

"I will ride a little ways," Teresa said. Her caution gave way to her exhaustion.

Buck helped her into the saddle and let her lead the way.

Once he was mounted, Buck fished around his saddlebag for the box of cartridges for the shells. In the saddle, he reloaded the Henry rifle. He stowed the cartridge box back in the saddlebag, but he held the Henry across his lap.

"That last volley of shots we heard, that was probably them making a charge on the cabin," Buck said. "I would guess they're inside now, and they've figured out that we made a run out the back."

"I thought so, too, when I heard it," Teresa said.

"They'll ransack the cabin. Don't you think?" Buck asked.

"They'll look for the loot," Teresa agreed.

"They won't come after us until they're satisfied

that the money is not there," Buck said.

"How long will that take?" Teresa asked.

"It's not a very big cabin," Buck said. "A quarter of an hour? Half an hour? Maybe not longer than that."

They rode on in silence for a long time. The trail was sometimes barely visible, so thick with forest growth. In places, it wasn't even much of a deer path. In other places, it opened up into a wider, more obvious path.

The fog was burning off and the sun had cleared the eastern peaks.

"We will come to a large, open grassland," Teresa said. "That is the pass, and when we reach the tree line again we will be on the eastern slope. But the open grassland is very large. Much, much bigger than the meadow in front of the cabin. If they have not caught us by the time we reach it, surely they will catch us there."

Buck turned in his saddle, watching for the pursuers.

He could not see the outlaws in pursuit, but he felt their presence in the lump in his throat.

"We just have to keep pressing," Buck said. "Every step gets us one step closer to safety."

- 9 -

When the trees evaporated and left the trail ahead nothing more than grassland and a high, rocky peak, Buck saw what Teresa meant.

The open space was immense. At the pace they were setting, it would take an hour to cross it, and here at the base of the peak the meadow curled around in such a way that you could see from west to east.

The grassland was littered with rocks and large boulders cropping up out of the ground, and that was some comfort because it meant that the Old Bunch couldn't race at a gallop and overtake them. They would have to be more careful here, in the open meadow, than they were along the wooded trail.

As he saw it, Buck began to formulate a plan.

He was a good shot with the Henry rifle. All those years spent hunting with his grandfather had made him a good shot. So far, he'd been at a disadvantage in every encounter with the Old Bunch.

Either they had the high ground on him or they

had sufficient cover or the need for hurry overcame the need for a well-placed shot.

But in this wide grassland at the top of the divide, Buck saw an opportunity.

"You keep riding," Buck said to Teresa. "Take the pack horse and keep going. Even if I never catch up to you, just keep going to Las Vegas."

"What are you going to do?" Teresa asked.

"I'm going to try to hold them off. I think I can make a stand here."

They did not quit riding as they talked.

Buck was looking for the right spot, and up ahead he thought he saw it.

A large outcropping of rocks formed a small cliff that pushed up toward the mountain peak. But there was space behind it where Buck could secret his horse and gain a concealed firing position. His field of fire would be open all the way to the tree line.

Teresa turned in her saddle to look at Buck.

"I do not want to go alone," she said.

"I'll catch up to you," Buck said. "You won't be alone for long."

Throughout the ordeal Buck had not seen worry in her eyes. But now she seemed truly worried. He did not know if her concern was for him or solely for herself, but Buck believed she felt some affection for him.

"Be careful," she said. "Hurry back to me."

Buck nodded.

Now he rode on ahead, up to the rocky

outcropping. While Teresa, now behind him on the trail and leading the packhorse, still came on at a walk, Buck made his preparations. He found a place to tie the gray where the mare would be out of sight, and he took out the box of cartridges.

In the outcropping, he found a good perch, a place where he could stand hidden from view down the trail.

As Teresa passed by, Buck called to her.

"You keep going. Even if you hear a gunfight, just keep going. Don't stop. If I can, I'll catch up to you. If I can't, I'll do my best to buy you time enough to keep going."

"I don't know how much farther I should keep riding," Teresa said. "It cannot be good for the baby."

Buck nodded. "Get beyond the clearing if you can. Back inside the far tree line. Then you can walk a ways. But now, while you can, get as much distance between you and them."

Left alone, Deputy Buckner began to contemplate what he was thinking of doing. When the notion struck him, he thought he was simply finding a way to stall the Old Bunch. But now his mind was turning over a single word. He was considering the implications of the word, all the things he'd ever heard anyone say about it, all the feelings that word conjured for him and others. And he had to wonder if a deputy marshal – a lawman – should even be contemplating what he was doing.

Ambush.

It was tactic of outlaws. Killers and highwaymen ambushed people. A dry-gulcher was no different than a backshooter. They were the lowest of the low.

Buckner's lip curled in disgust as he considered the types of people who would commit an ambush.

He wondered if a lawman, protecting an innocent woman, could ambush outlaws in good conscience. But his intuition told him that he was simply trying to justify the inexcusable.

But he made a promise, and whether he was a lawman or not, a man's honor didn't allow him to give a promise lightly. And right now, Deputy Buckner felt the weight of that promise more than he felt the oath he took as a deputy.

Besides, the Old Bunch – and any new members now riding with them – were wanted men, and the law didn't make a distinction with these killers whether they were taken alive or dead.

The curled lip turned from disgust to contempt as Buckner remembered how the Old Bunch had done their own ambush, killing off good citizens who agreed to ride with the posse.

And they had also killed Rick Compton without giving him a chance. And they'd shot a man who was bound in shackles and unarmed.

Buck lowered the lever slightly on the Henry rifle to be sure a round was chambered.

Then he set his eyes firmly on his backtrail, and he waited for the Old Bunch to emerge from the tree line.

***

Rusty and Dick Hale and the two men riding with them emerged from the tree line more than an hour after Buck had secured his position behind the rocky outcropping.

It took them so long to appear, that Buck was beginning to hope that they might have been unable to find the trail and could not track him and Teresa.

But that hope was gone, now.

Even from a distance, Buck could distinguish which ones were the Hale brothers.

He'd seen Rusty Hale with the Colt revolving rifle the previous day, so he knew which one was Rusty. But Dick Hale favored his brother, even rode a horse like him. Also, the two men with them were younger – obviously younger. The one in the back, leading the spare horses, he wasn't more than a boy. The other one was about Buck's age, and he was the man riding out front now.

They were riding at a slow walk, and the younger man up front seemed to be watching for tracks.

Buck's hat was sitting on the mare's saddle horn, and he kept back in the shadows behind the outcropping, just putting enough of his head out to watch them.

In the time spent waiting for them to appear on the trail, Buck had already picked his spot. There was a slight incline along the path. The horses would have to pause to make that step up. That would give Buck the best chance of making sure his first shot hit a target.

He did not know how the Old Bunch would respond.

They might drop from their horses, and Buck would be in a shootout. He'd already decided this was preferable. If he could seriously wound or kill one man with his first shot, he could shoot it out all afternoon with the others. Even if he never shot one of them, it would buy Teresa a considerable amount of time. And the chances were good that he could get at least one more in a shooting match. Buck was a good shot.

But Red Hogan said they were in the war. Buck didn't know if they were cavalrymen or foot soldiers. Cavalrymen might charge. If they came on at a gallop, Buck knew he would be hard pressed to shoot another one, and they would likely end this thing pretty soon. No shootout. No standoff.

As he watched him, he saw that Kirby Hale's arm was bandaged. Buck thought when he took a shot at him yesterday that he'd hit Kirby in the arm. The bandaged appeared to be confirmation of that.

He also thought he'd hit one of them in the meadow outside of Red Hogan's cabin. But he did not see any other bandages on any of them.

The front man was nearing the slight incline. Buck had already decided, before he ever saw them, that he'd have to shoot to kill the man in front. If he let one pass that incline, that man would likely be more apt to make a charge.

Whatever happened, Buck didn't want this to be over fast. His goal in making this ambush was to give Teresa as much time as he could. He was even willing to stay here until dark, knowing that dark would give them a chance to get up close to him.

Buck took a breath.

There was no second chance on this. There was no thinking about it. When the moment came, he had no choice now but to act.

The gray mare behind him lifted her head, smelling the other horses nearby.

Buck slowly raised the Henry rifle.

The front man's horse paused as it started to take the step.

Buck looked down the barrel through the sights.

He let out a breath and squeezed the trigger.

He'd stood so long in the quiet of the mountain that the Henry rifle seemed like a powder keg as it thundered out its report.

The front rider jerked and fell back, dragging the reins. His horse reared and then toppled as the man fell backwards from the saddle, the horse landing on top of the rider.

It must have been the stillness of the quiet mountain trail, but the horses all spooked.

The horses in the Old Bunch's small remuda all reared and jerked, pulling loose from the rider who was trailing them, and they turned and bolted back down the back trail.

The mounts weren't much better, dancing their agitation as the riders tried to get them under control.

Buck decided to feed the panic.

He dropped the lever on the Henry and fired another shot. The horses were all bucking too much for any shot to tell, but it was enough to send more fear into the horses.

To get their mounts under control, the Hale brothers had to turn and ride away from danger.

Buck dropped the lever on the Henry again and took aim. With their backs exposed and the horse now running instead of rearing, Deputy Buckner looked down the barrel and knew he could shoot Dick Hale in the back. The shot was there. He had it. But the deputy marshal's finger stayed off the trigger.

He was sure his first shot had given the lead rider a mortal wound, though the man was not yet dead.

Killing a man in ambush was one thing, but Buck couldn't bring himself to shoot a man in the back.

When the three remaining men of the Old Bunch had cleared the tree line, Buckner fired the Henry.

He'd not considered that they might flee. His planning was all about whether they would dismount and fight or charge his position.

But as soon as the three riders were back among the trees, Buck decided to run.

He slid down from his perch and snatched at the gray's reins, pulling them loose from where he'd hitched the horse to a bush. And fast, he was in the saddle and spurring the horse forward.

A couple of unenthusiastic shots followed him as horse and rider emerged from behind the outcropping of rocks. But Buck was already out of range, and the mare was gathering speed quickly, even over the rocky terrain.

Buck held his breath with each fall of the hoofs, praying that the horse did not stumble and spill on a loose rock.

He chanced a look over his shoulder and saw no one there. Whatever was happening back behind him, the outlaws were not pursuing immediately.

Buck felt it as the slight slope at the top of the mountain ridge dipped and began to descend. He'd crossed the divide and was on the eastern slope now. He chanced another look, but he was rounding the rocky peak and his backtrail was out of sight now.

Ahead of him, but a good distance down the slope, the big pines rose up, and Buck searched the tree line for the trail.

The mare began to slow, and Buck checked over his shoulder again. Still no pursuit.

They might be tending to the injured man. That could keep them some time. They might also be going after the panicked horses. Again, that could buy Buck and Teresa a lot of time.

As the meadow narrowed into a natural draw, Buck thought he saw a gap in the tree line. It was the sort of hole he'd seen a thousand times in a stand of trees where branches were stunted and no undergrowth grew because the deer and elk followed the natural trails and had tramped down all the undergrowth and broken branches on saplings.

Buck reined in, bringing the horse to a walk. Only a fool would ride hard into a tree line. A low branch might do the job for the Old Bunch.

In the woods the natural trail was easy enough to follow. Deer and elk probably tracked this path daily, seeking water and the safety of thick cover. They trampled down the undergrowth, and marked a clear trail. Buck kept the horse at an easy trot, picking out the path as he went and dodging low branches that would never trouble a deer or elk but would knock a mounted man from his saddle.

Whatever else he had done, Deputy Buckner had bought Teresa more time to put a wider distance between her and the Old Bunch. But also, he had bettered the odds. Now Buck only had to protect Teresa from just the two Hale brothers and the one boy who so far had done nothing more than lead the horses.

- 10 -

"Buck," Teresa said, rolling the name around in her mouth. "Buck Buckner. Is that your name?"

Buck chuckled.

"Naw, folks just call me Buck on account of it being short for Buckner. They called my granddaddy 'Buck' and they called my pa 'Buck,' and now they call me 'Buck.'"

Teresa narrowed her eyes.

"So what is your name?"

"Gideon," Buck told her. "My name is Gideon Buckner. My mama was the only one ever called me that, though."

Teresa laughed, and for the first time since he'd met her, Buck saw her eyes smile.

"I can understand why you prefer Buck over Gideon. I think you are right to stay with Buck."

"Yes, ma'am," Buck answered with a grin.

The cave was really more of a rocky overhang than a cave. As far as Buck could tell, it did not go much more than thirty feet deep. But it was enclosed on three sides and the overhang and scrub oak growth all around kept it well hidden from view.

When Buck at last caught up with Teresa on the deer path, he was impressed at the distance she had covered on foot. It took him more than two hours to catch up to her.

They pressed on for another hour, out through a grassy meadow and back into a forest that hugged a rocky peak. It was here at the base of the peak that Buck found the cave, and what made it ideal was that it offered a view of the meadow. He did not see the cave, either from the meadow or the trail through the woods, but he suspected there might be a cave, or something like it, at the base of the peak. And so he led Teresa off the trail.

"We'll stop here for the night," Buck said. "You can rest, and I will keep a watch."

"It's too early to stop," Teresa argued. "There's still three or four hours of daylight."

"I know," Buck said. "And you're not wrong. But I don't reckon we'll find a better place to camp. We can hitch the horses at the back of the cave. And I can watch the meadow. The worst part about having them behind us is not knowing where they are."

So Teresa agreed.

She made herself a pallet of blankets and she sat on that. But sleep did not come easily, and so now she talked to Deputy Buckner.

"How long have you been a deputy marshal?" Teresa asked.

"About three months. But before that I worked for the marshal, running errands and messages for him, sweeping up his office and things of that nature. So when one of his deputies quit to go to the silver mines, I asked for the job."

"What made you want to be a marshal?" Teresa asked.

Buck shrugged.

Teresa's bed was at one side of the cave, and Buck was leaning against the opposite wall where he could watch the meadow.

"Something to do," he said. "My pa was a lawman back in Arkansas. He was killed in a gunfight with a horse thief."

"How old were you?"

Buck thought about it. "I guess I was about thirteen years old when my pa was killed. After that, me and my ma lived with my granddaddy and his wife. She was granddaddy's second wife, and not my real grandmother. I never knew my real grandmother."

"Was that in Santa Fe?"

Buck laughed. "No, not in Santa Fe. That was back in Arkansas. That's where all my people come from. I come out to New Mexico Territory a couple of years ago, working on a wagon train. I left the train at Fort Union and stayed there for a while, and then I made my way over to Santa Fe. Took some jobs until I finally went to work for the marshal."

Teresa studied his face as he watched the meadow.

"You are a very good outdoorsman," she said.

"I spent a lot of time in the woods of the Ozarks with my granddaddy," Buck said. "We hunted and fished just about all the time. He had a little brewery and tavern, and by the time I come along my uncles were running that. So he didn't have nothing better to do than teach me to hunt deer and squirrel and find good caves for making a camp."

Buck smiled thinking about his grandfather and the days spent camping in the wilderness.

"Everybody always said he was going to make me part Injun, but we had a good time. We had better caves back in Arkansas than there are here, though."

"If you like caves," Teresa said.

"What about you? Have you always lived in New Mexico Territory?"

Teresa shifted her position. Though she had three blankets down, she was still sitting on the hard, rock floor, and she was very uncomfortable.

"My people were in Las Vegas when this was all still Mexico," she said. "When the war came and the United States took it over, we stayed. One government does not make much difference than another."

Buck looked at her in the fading light of evening. She was a striking woman, even pregnant like she was. He found himself feeling jealous of Red Hogan, and wondering how such a loathsome man could deserve to have such a beautiful woman. But he remembered, too, what Teresa had said to Red as they were taking him off. She said she never loved him.

"How come you stayed with Red?"

Teresa smiled her sad smile.

"Being with Red was better than anything else I've ever done."

"But you didn't love him?"

"He was fun," Teresa said. "When I knew him in Las Vegas, he was full of fun all the time. When we first came to the mountains and were building the cabin, I would say we were happy. But that was no life for him, and he got bored of it."

"Was it a life for you?" Buck asked. "Living alone with Red Hogan in a mountain cabin?"

Teresa shrugged.

"Life is life. I preferred what I had at the cabin to what I had in Las Vegas."

"What will you do now?" Buck asked.

Teresa shook her head.

"Probably these men will kill me."

"I ain't gonna let that happen," Buck said. "I promised Red I would get you out of this. He wants you to take that money and go east. He wants you to use that money to raise your baby to be decent. He made me swear I would see to it that you did."

"It costs a lot of money to go east," Teresa said.

"The loot," Buck said. "Do you know how much it is?"

Teresa shook her head.

"Forty thousand dollars, is what Red told me."

Teresa drew back in surprise, her eyes wide.

"He wants you to go to Chicago or some other place back east to raise your child, and he wants you to use that money to do it."

Buck did not tell Teresa that Red Hogan had promised him half of the loot. He never intended to take any of it anyway.

"Can it really be so much?" Teresa asked, her voice hardly more audible than her breath.

"That's what Red told me," Buck said. "I reckon he didn't have cause to lie about it."

"He always told me that when things settled down we would never have to worry about money. He said we could go anywhere in the world we wanted. But I never knew it was so much money."

Buck looked back out at the meadow. Still he'd seen nothing of the Hale brothers. He could not believe that they had given up the chase.

"What will we do if they come into the meadow after dark?" Teresa asked. "They could get in front of us."

Buck nodded.

"I would almost prefer that," he said. "I'm a fair hand at tracking, and if they were in front of us at least I could know where they are. But with them behind us, they could catch us at any time."

"What is taking them so long to catch us?" Teresa asked.

"I shot one of them back there and scattered their horses. I reckon that was enough to delay them."

"Maybe they won't keep coming," Teresa said hopefully.

Buck grinned.

"I reckon they've got forty thousand good reasons

to keep coming," he said.

"Why are you doing this?"

"Doing what?" Buck said.

"You came back to the cabin for me. You're helping me along. You're risking your life for me. Why?"

Buck ran the toe of his boot through the thin layer of sand covering the rock at his feet.

"It's the right thing to do," Buck said. "You're a woman, and you need help. So it's just right. But also, other than that, I promised Red I would come back for you and get you out of all this. He'd been shot twice and was dying. And where I come from, if you make a man a promise that's a debt you owe him. But especially a dying man. And so I reckon I'm just paying my debt."

***

Deputy Buckner dozed some through the night, and for a brief while he laid down on Teresa's blankets and slept while Teresa sat up and listened for movement in the woods. When the first blue light of dawn touched the night sky, Buck packed what he could of their supplies and saddled the horses, waiting until the last moment to wake Teresa.

A fog drifted through the trees, and Buck could not see into the meadow to know if the Old Bunch were there or not.

"I'd like to work our way through the woods and stay off that deer path," Buck said. "The deer path guarantees us a route. The animals know how to get lower, down to the valley creeks and forage. But it's also an easy trail to follow, and the Old Bunch will surely follow that."

"Red never talked about any other trail. It was just the one that goes to the village of Rociada. And I know that from Rociada we can travel through a valley directly down to Las Vegas. If we leave the draw and the deer path, won't we risk getting lost?"

"We risk it," he said. "But we're trying to lose the Old Bunch. We're trying to throw Dick and Rusty Hale off our path. The best way I know to lose someone who's following you is to get lost yourself. If we don't know where we are, they'll have a harder time following us."

Buck took the leads of the gray mare and the pack horse and started to trek south off the trail.

"You'll just have to trust me. It's better that we don't follow that same path," he said.

And so they set out through the forest. Buck relied on his instincts in the woods – instincts honed from years of reading draws and contours of the land, understanding how a ridge will likely drop to a creek, and how a dry creek will run to a river and a river will cut to a valley.

They picked their way slowly through undergrowth, sometimes have to backtrack to get around thickets or find a draw that would allow them to reach gentler slopes.

The fog lifted into the treetops and then burned off completely, and the day turned warmer.

They stopped at times so that Teresa could rest, but she only took short breaks. Through wide meadows they mounted and rode the horses, but where they were going there were too many low branches to ride.

In clearings or on high ground, Buck found the peak they had camped beneath and saw that they made little progress at first. But as the morning turned to afternoon, the peak was farther in the distance. And then he could no longer see the peak, even from a high ridge.

They crossed three small creeks that probably ran dry half the year but now had small streams. Each creek ran down into valleys that made the hills like fingers reaching to the east. The valleys each opened into wide meadows, and Buck was reluctant to drop down into the valley meadows for fear they would eventually run into each other.

"Even if we've left the Old Bunch behind and sent them down the wrong trail, we could wander right into them by accident if all these valleys connect together. At some point we'll reach a valley that will drop farther south, and that's the one we'll follow."

By late afternoon they reached another small creek that followed down a long draw.

"We'll follow this creek," Buck said.

Many years later, Teresa Hogan would come back into these hills and she would discover their mistake. They were one hill away from the Sapello River valley – a long, narrow valley that stretched far to the east and ran south to a pass that would have put them out of the mountains just a few miles north of Las Vegas. The discovery of it, and the memory of what was lost because she and Deputy Buckner followed the creek, caused her great heartache. But the heartache was bittersweet because no man can say what might lie down one path or another, and the joy Teresa Hogan discovered at becoming a mother and raising the son of an outlaw into a good and honest man might have been missed had she taken some other path.

The creek followed a long draw before it spilled out into a long valley, and that night Buckner and Teresa camped at the edge of the tree line.

They could see that the valley meadow stretched far around the hills.

"We'll be exposed in the valley," Buck said. "It's better to camp inside the trees. We'll have less walking tomorrow. We'll be able to mount up and ride through the valley. The horses can take it easy in the meadow."

Teresa made no argument. Her feet were sore, her thighs burned, and her ankles were terribly swollen and painful.

Buck unpacked the pannier and laid out the blankets on a bed of pine needles, and Teresa sat there.

He hitched the horses near to Teresa's bedroll while she slid out of her moccasins and rubbed the swelling down her swollen ankles.

"Gideon Buckner," Teresa said. "It's not so bad a name when you start to get accustomed to it."

Buck laughed.

"It looks fine enough on a tombstone," Buck said. "I've seen it on one twice."

"Your father and grandfather?" Teresa asked.

"That's right," Buck said. "They both wear their names on their tombstones with some pride. Good men, wise and strong, who left behind people who loved them. But it's a tough sort of name to tote around while you're alive."

"It's better than Jerubbaal," Teresa said.

Buck looked at her with surprise and laughed. "Yes, I reckon that it is. You're a Christian woman?"

"I was raised to go to church on Sunday by an aunt and uncle who did their best Monday through Saturday to make a mockery of Sunday.

"That's too bad," Buck said.

"Were you brought up in the church?"

Buck laughed.

"There wasn't a church near us that you could get to on Sunday mornings," Buck said. "Not in the Ozarks. So our church was my grandmama's knee, and she taught us to read from the Bible."

They ate a supper of cold jerky and biscuits.

"It's not much for a pregnant woman, but we'll get you fed proper as soon as we're in Las Vegas," Buck said.

"I'll be fine," Teresa said. "I'm not here for the luxuries."

The shadows of the trees reached far into the valley meadow now, and the air was growing chilly again. They made no fire for fear that it might lead the Old Bunch gang to them if, somehow, the Hale brothers had managed to pick up their trail.

Buck grew silent after supper. Unlike the previous night, he did not have a meadow to watch. Keeping a lookout meant simply listening for sounds in the woods.

"What bothers you, Gideon Buckner?" Teresa asked, taking the liberty of using Buck's given name.

Buck smiled at her, but Teresa recognized a smile

with no warmth.

"I'm just thinking about Deputy Compton," Buck said. "And Red, too. I left both of them out there on the Pecos trail. Rick Compton was shot and dead, and Red was dying. And I don't reckon that the Old Bunch thought much of burying them. And I'm thinking when this is done I should go back and bury them. It would be the decent thing to do."

Teresa shrugged.

"I expect Red always figured he'd die on a trail somewhere and just be left to rot. I can't speak for Deputy Compton."

"A man should have a stone with his name on it," Buck said.

"Even a man like Red?" Teresa asked.

"Even a man like Red. He might not have been a good man, but he was good to you. Wasn't he?"

"He never hit me," Teresa said. "He gave me a better life than the one I had. I suppose he was good to me."

"I'd just hate to think of being left in a place without a decent burial and no stone that says I was a man."

Teresa pulled a blanket up tight around her.

"I'll spell you if you'll wake me after a while," Teresa said.

Buck stretched and buttoned his coat closed.

"I might do that," he said.

The night turned dark and the only noises Buck heard were the ones that should have been there. A hoot owl somewhere nearby seemed perturbed that Buck and Teresa had interrupted his hunting grounds, but as he listened he heard the owl move from the woods to the meadow and knew the owl had found itself a midnight snack.

Buck knew the horses would prove to be the best harbinger of trouble, but they stayed quiet through the night.

With only a couple of hours left to daylight, Buck leaned against the slope of the draw and closed his eyes.

- 11 -

Teresa Hogan abandoned her caution over riding.

They mounted as soon as they left the tree line and entered into the valley meadow, and Teresa no longer was adamant that she must walk for the sake of her unborn baby.

Through the morning they continued to follow the creek as it led them through a long, flat canyon. The canyon was so narrow it was difficult to see anything beyond the immediate hills, and Buck could not judge based on the peaks exactly how they were traveling. But the sun's position gave him cause for concern.

"We should be heading more east and south," Buck said. "But this valley seems to be taking us back up to the northeast."

"Is that a problem?" Teresa asked.

"I've never been in these hills before, but it stands to reason that all these little valleys and canyons are going to eventually meet somewhere. If they meet east of the mountains and drop south, that's fine. But if they meet somewhere in the mountains, we could easily be headed to the same trail the Hale brothers are following. I had thought we'd gone far enough south to avoid them, but I'm not sure, now."

"Should we turn back?" Teresa asked.

Buck let out a soft whistle.

"Maybe so," he said. "I don't like the way this valley seems to be running. If we do turn back, we're probably two days from Las Vegas instead of one."

He watched Teresa Hogan's face as he said it, and he could see that she was pained at the thought of another day, whether it was in the saddle or on foot.

"Or maybe no," Buck said, and he was certain he saw relief in her face.

"At this point, we've got no reason to think the Hale brothers are still behind us. Which means they don't know where we are any more than we know where we are. Maybe they turned back. Or maybe they pushed on ahead to Las Vegas. But they won't stay there. They're just as wanted as Red in Las Vegas."

Teresa laughed.

"You do not know Las Vegas, do you?" she asked.

"Not well," Buck said. "I spent some time at Fort Union, but not much time around Las Vegas."

"Every man in Las Vegas is wanted," Teresa said.

"Maybe," Buck said. "But I still don't reckon they'll be much trouble for us there. They have big bounties on them, and there are lawmen in Las Vegas. I just don't reckon they'll stay there over long. So we'll follow this canyon where it leads, and if it happens to meet up with the same valley that the Old Bunch are in, and if they happen to be there the same time we get there, then we'll have it out with them then."

Teresa was visibly relieved.

"Do you want to walk a ways?" Buck asked her.

"No," she said. "My feet and back are so sore. My thighs are burning from all the walking yesterday. But I think it is probably best if we walk for a while."

They saw a small herd of pronghorn leap from the forest in front of them and bound into the meadow. The pronghorn stopped and grazed in front of them, oblivious or unconcerned about the man and woman walking alongside three horses.

"If I weren't worried about someone hearing the shot, we'd have fresh meat for supper," Buck said.

"Could you shoot one at this distance?" Teresa asked.

"Probably not," Buck said honestly. "But we get forty yards closer and I could."

Before they'd cleared the distance, though, the pronghorn retreated back into the cover of the trees.

A while later they watched a hawk swoop in to hunt mice in the meadow.

"What will you do when we reach Las Vegas?" Teresa asked.

"I've been thinking on that," Buck said. "I promised Red that I would get you out of the mountains safe and see to it that you took that baby and went east. He wanted you raising the baby in a decent, safe place. So I figure I'll help you dig up that stolen loot, and once you've got it, I'll put you on a stagecoach east. Wherever you want to go. And once you're safe and away, I'll follow the stagecoach back to Santa Fe."

"What if I do not want to go east?" Teresa said.

"Where would you want to go?"

"Maybe to Santa Fe," Teresa said. "If you wanted, I would go with you."

Buck chuckled. "Santa Fe ain't nothin'. Why would you want to go there?"

"It's not Santa Fe that would make me go. It's you."

Buck glanced at her, and then he took a second look, a longer look. Teresa was looking at him, and somewhere under the sadness he typically found in her eyes was something else. Deputy Buckner did not have the word for what it was, but a better educated man would have called it a "seductive look."

All the same, Buck knew how that look made him feel.

"Why would you want to go with me?" Buck asked.

"Because you're kind, and considerate," Teresa said. "You're so many things that Buck was not. Since I met you, I've thought that I could have spent the rest of my life in that mountain cabin with you and nobody but you."

Buck glanced at her swollen belly.

"I reckon it wouldn't just be me," he said.

Teresa dropped her eyes.

"No," she said. "And if you would not have a pregnant woman, I could not blame you. Not many men would have an interest in raising another man's baby."

"Oh, it ain't that," Buck said. "I reckon that wouldn't bother me. I'm just saying it would never be just me and you in that cabin."

"Would you have me in Santa Fe?" Teresa asked.

Buck's face turned red, and he felt the embarrassment in his cheeks.

"I reckon," he started, but the words got lost as he fumbled for his thoughts. "I guess what I mean to say. Well, ma'am, I'd be proud."

Teresa smiled.

"You're very sweet, Gideon Buckner," she said.

Buck did not know what else to say, so he just said, "Yes, ma'am."

They went on through the late morning, and with the sun directly overhead they at last came to a place where the canyon meadow began to widen and the hill to their north started to drop.

"Up ahead," Buck said. "We're like as not to find out where we are. That's a bigger valley there."

Now Buck pulled the horses to a stop and picketed them so that they could graze a bit in the meadow. He put out a blanket for Teresa to sit on and gave her some food. And then he checked their weapons.

"Are you worried?" Teresa said as Buck broke open the top of the double barrel shotgun to ensure that there were shells in it.

"Not worried," he said. "But if we're going to see the Hale brothers again, it could be in that valley we're about to walk into."

He checked his Henry rifle and his Colt Army. He

blew into the Henry's ejection port and banged the receiver against the palm of his hand a few times, hoping to kick out any dust and sand that might have gotten trapped in there. The last thing he needed was his rifle to jam.

They were exposed now in the canyon, but Buck felt safe. If the Old Bunch came at them now, they would have to come through the mouth of the canyon, and Buck would see them coming a mile away.

The sun was warm, and Buck laid down in the grass and dozed a bit while Teresa rested.

And then they packed up the blanket, stowed the weapons back on the horses, and resumed their walk.

As they came out into the wider valley, they saw a shallow river running through it. The river ran quick and clear as glass. The grass in the meadow was tall. But right through the middle of the valley a clear and obvious path was beat down to dirt, littered with the tracks of shod horses and wagon wheels.

And not far to the north of where their canyon entered the wider valley they saw a small cluster of buildings.

"Let's go find out where we are," Buck said. "Maybe someone there can rent us a wagon or give us a meal."

Teresa looked up and down the valley as they started toward the buildings. Something about it felt familiar to her. But it wasn't until they were in the tiny village that Teresa realized she had been here before.

She put out a hand on Buck's shoulder and said, "Deputy Buckner, I know this place. This is Rociada."

- 12 -

They hitched the horses outside a small cantina on the plaza. To call it a plaza was overly generous. There was a small grassy courtyard with a patch of dirt in the middle. The courtyard was square, and there were a handful of buildings around it. A couple of houses. A saloon and the cantina. A church at one end. All of the buildings stood alone, and it was nothing like a real plaza. But it was what Rociada had to offer.

Buck and Teresa walked together into the cantina.

A man sat in a chair at the back of the cantina, his head leaned against the wall. The cantina was well lit from all the open windows on the sides and at the front. The building ran deep to the back, and only half of it was occupied by the cantina. A hallway against one wall ran to the back, and Buck guessed the proprietor's residence was in the back, and maybe a room or two to let.

The cantina smelled of fried steak, onion, and peppers. Red and green peppers hung in bunches, and there was a kitchen behind the bar.

Other than the man asleep in the chair, there was no one else inside the cantina.

"Do you have food?" Buck asked.

The startled man jumped in his chair and then hurriedly got to his feet.

"Ha," he chuckled. "You caught me napping, amigo."

"Food?" Buck asked again.

"Oh, si. Of course. We have steak and beans."

"Do you have beer?" Buck asked.

"We have beer," the man said happily.

"Two beers and two plates," Buck said, digging in a pocket for his coins.

"Is this Rociada?" Buck asked.

"Si, this is Rociada," the man said.

"How far to Las Vegas from here?"

"Las Vegas is thirty miles from here," the man said, walking behind the bar to get two mugs of beer.

Buck and Teresa sat at a table near the back of the cantina where Buck had a good view of the door and could see the horses through a window.

"Don't sit between me and the door," Buck said to Teresa. "Slide that chair around and sit closer to me."

"Have you had any strangers pass through?" Buck asked.

"Strangers?" the man said as he dished beans onto two plates. "You are the first strangers I have seen in a number of days. We do not often have a man and his wife pass through here. Particularly when his wife is pregnant."

Buck did not correct the man.

"Do you have a livery stable here?" Buck asked.

The man walked from the stove over to the table where Buck and Teresa sat. He set down the plates in front of them.

"There is a stable and corral down at the end of town. It is Senor Baca's stable and corral, but he opens it up to strangers who stop here. For a fee, of course."

"Does he rent wagons or buggies?" Buck asked.

"Oh, no," the man said. "He does not rent wagons."

"Does anyone in town rent wagons? My wife is very tired. Riding is not good for the baby, and her feet are sore from too much walking."

The man shook his head.

"I am sorry, amigo. No one in Rociada rents wagons. Are you trying to get to Las Vegas?"

"Yes, we are," Buck said. "Do you rent rooms here?"

"I do," the man said happily. "But both of my rooms are occupied."

Buck gave him a quizzical look.

"I thought you said you'd had no strangers through here," Buck said.

The man laughed happily. "The Hale brothers are no strangers."

A noise in the hallway that led to the back of the cantina caught everyone's attention, and all three of them looked at the entrance to the hall where a man had just walked in from the back.

"Ah, there is Senor Dick Hale now," the cantina man said. "Perhaps, to free up one room, Senor Dick might share a room with Senor Rusty."

Deputy Marshal Gideon Buckner was no gunfighter, at least not in that sense. He could shoot an elk from distance, or – as he had learned in recent days – a man if he had to. But he was not the sort of man who drew fast inside a cantina and fired off a round before his opponent could clear leather.

But he did have an advantage over Dick Hale in that Buckner knew immediately that Hale was his adversary, and Dick Hale, having just walked into the cantina's dining room, did not realize the quarry he sought was right in front of him.

Buck jumped up from his chair, and it fell backwards with a loud crash.

Buck reached across himself with his left hand to clear the leather thong from the hammer of his Colt while dragging the revolver from its holster with his right hand.

Now his advantage ended.

"Rusty!" Dick Hale shouted.

Dick Hale was a gunfighter, and as Buck brought his Colt army level, Dick Hale already had his gun out of the holster.

Both six-shooters fired simultaneously. Buck's slight advantage gave him a half second more to get his gun on target, though he never really aimed.

Dick Hale's bullet cut a gash on the outside of Buck's thigh. The deputy marshal felt the tear at his leg, but in the moment, with his dander up in the sudden violence, it didn't feel like anything other than someone tugging on his pants.

Buck's bullet did more damage to its intended victim. Dick Hale's neck opened up, and his eyes grew wide as he realized he'd been shot in the throat. It was not the pain of the injury, but the immediate recognition of its seriousness that caused Dick Hale to drop his gun and reach with both hands to try to stop the bleeding at his neck.

Buckner thumbed back the hammer of the revolver and fired a second shot. This one was better aimed, and it smashed into Hale's chest.

Hale dropped to his knees and then collapsed in the hallway.

"Run to the horses," Buck said to Teresa, and he was surprised by the calmness of his voice. "Ride out of here as fast as you can."

He thumbed back the hammer again, and a door down the hallway opened. A man peered out, and Buck immediately recognized Rusty Hale.

Buck fired a shot that splinted the door frame near Rusty Hale's head, and Rusty ducked back inside the room.

The man from the cantina fled behind his bar.

Buck cocked back the hammer and let loose another bullet that hit the door frame a second time.

He gave a look for the man from the cantina who had disappeared behind the bar, but he kept his Colt pointed down the hallway.

Now, slowly, Buck started to back away toward the door.

Dick Hale's body lay motionless on the ground in the hallway. Buck was fairly sure he'd killed that man. There was a younger man somewhere – the one who'd been toting the spare horses the whole time. Buck was not certain where he was, and the lawman worried that the boy might appear in the doorway behind him. He didn't want to be caught between Rusty Hale and someone else at the door.

Teresa was making tracks out of the town and into the valley. She'd grabbed the lead on the pack horse when she mounted up on her own horse.

As he moved backwards through the cantina, Buck started to limp. That was the first time he realized he'd been shot. He glanced down at the wound and saw a tear in his pants and a moist stain. His leg stung, but the wound was only on the surface.

Buck started to think about how he might escape.

If he got on his horse and rode fast he could be outside of easy rifle shot probably before Rusty Hale had a chance to follow him out the door of the cantina.

Then the pursuit would be renewed.

Buck glanced over his shoulder to see where Teresa had gone. She was well outside of the cluster of ramshackle buildings that served as a town.

When he looked back, Buck saw Rusty Hale starting out of the door again. Buck squeezed the trigger on his Colt, and the gunshot was enough to back Rusty Hale into the room.

That was five shots. The Colt was empty.

Most everyone knew to keep the cylinder below the hammer empty to prevent accidental discharge when the gun was in a holster, and only a few daring souls didn't do that. Buck wasn't that daring.

But now he was sitting on empty.

Quickly, he slid six rounds out of his belt and into his hand. He never lowered the gun in case Rusty Hale peered around the edge of the door frame again.

Ejecting the empty casings was going to make noise, and Buck knew when Rusty Hale heard those casings hit the floor he was going to come out of that door shooting.

"Rusty Hale!" Buck called at the hallway. "You throw out your guns and come through that doorway with your hands up. I'm a deputy marshal from Santa Fe, and I'm going to take you in."

There was silence for a moment. And then Hale responded.

"You ain't takin' nobody nowhere," Rusty Hale said. "I want that girl."

Buck dropped to one knee, held the Colt close to the ground, opened the gate and began ejecting each of the spent casings from the cylinder. With the Colt near the ground the casings did not make so much noise, and Rusty Hale was continuing to talk. The sound of his own voice drowned out the noise of the casings.

"I just need to talk to her. We wasn't gonna do her nor you no harm. But now you done killed my brother, and I ain't got no choice but to do for you. And when I have done, I'm going to go fetch up that girl and do for her, too."

"You throw out your gun and you won't end up shot dead like your brother," Buck said.

Rusty Hale stuck the gun out the doorway, but he twisted his wrist and without looking fired a shot that made Buck drop his head. It was a blind shot that flew harmlessly into the wall. But Rusty followed it around the door frame, thumbing back the hammer and firing off a second shot. This one was better placed and narrowly missed Buck, who was still kneeling at the floor.

Buck fired a shot in return, but his aim was off. Even with Rusty Hale filling up the narrow hallway, Buck missed his target.

The deputy marshal sprang to his feet and made for the door of the cantina, but his balance was off and he fell into a table and chairs before righting himself. As he stumbled toward the door, Buck twisted and fired a wild shot at the hallway. It didn't hit Rusty, but it was enough to back him up.

Buck snatched at the lead hitching his mare to a post and pointed his gun at the cantina's open window. He stepped into the stirrup and before wheeling the horse to start down the road he fired off one more shot into the cantina. There was nothing to aim at. Rusty Hale was outside of his view, but Buck hoped a last shot would keep back the surviving Hale brother long enough for the gray mare to get some speed worked up.

***

As he left the dirt track that served as Rociada's main thoroughfare, Buck heard a shot fired from the cantina. But he was already out of range and the gray mare was galloping hard into the meadow.

He was surprised at how far ahead Teresa and the packhorse had managed to get.

Buck's heart was pounding in his chest. With the enthusiasm of youth, he felt enormous excitement at having just faced off in a gunfight with two known killers, wanted men, and survived it. Not only had he survived it, but he'd killed one of the Hale brothers. The Old Bunch gang were notorious. Buck, of course, had never faced them before as a lawman, but the other deputy marshals all talked about the Old Bunch gang and the massacre of the posse.

And Buck had now killed one of the actual members of the gang. Not some new addition to the Old Bunch, but a known man. Dick Hale.

Buck's excitement was almost enough to make him wheel his horse and go back to face Rusty Hale again. But in the distance, looking very small, was a woman who Buck had promised to see to safety, and right now catching up to Teresa Hogan was most important to him.

Buck looked over his shoulder at the little village he was leaving behind, and he saw no sign of pursuit.

After several minutes, Teresa's horse started to slow.

The gray mare was up to the challenge, though, and kept her gallop going until at last catching up to Teresa, who now had her horse at a walk.

"Rusty Hale is still back there," Buck told her.

"Is he chasing us?" Teresa asked, turning her horse sideways rather than trying to twist in the saddle.

"He will be, but not yet," Buck said.

"Did you kill that other man?" Teresa asked. "The one you shot?"

"That was Dick Hale," Buck said. "One of the Hale brothers of the Old Bunch. He's dead now."

Teresa noticed the blood on Buck's leg.

"Are you hurt bad?" she asked.

Buck glanced down at the ripped pants.

"I don't think so," he said.

Holding the reins in his teeth, Buck ripped a bigger hole in his pants and examined the wound.

"It's not so bad," he said through the reins. "It stings like the devil, but not so bad."

The valley was wide and flat, and the surrounding hills were pushing them back toward the north. Up ahead, though, the valley dropped in elevation and curved back south.

"This is the road to Las Vegas," Teresa said. "I remember coming through here with Red when we first went out to the mountains. We came through here leading a team of pack mules. All the tools Red needed to build the cabin, all the provisions we had with us to survive those first few months were loaded onto those mules. Red made a couple of trips to Rociada for supplies, or down to the stagecoach station on the Pecos. I remember coming through here and being very scared, as we got higher into the mountains, that all our provisions were loaded on the backs of a team of mules. I wondered how we would survive."

"It was a big chance to take. Are you glad you did it?" Buck asked.

"Who's to say?" Teresa asked.

As the road's elevation continued to drop, the trees seemed to tumble down out of the hills and close in on the roadway. Soon they were riding through a forest again, though here the road was clearly defined and cut a wide path, with enough for wagons and carts.

"We cannot make it to Las Vegas before dark," Buck said. "I never saw the other man that was with the Hale brothers. I don't know if he was in the room in the cantina or if he was somewhere else. But we know at least Rusty Hale will be behind us. And possibly he will have someone else with him."

"Should we leave the trail again?" Teresa asked.

Buck looked at their surroundings. They were riding through a thick pine forest that sometimes opened up into wide meadows dotted with juniper. Sometimes they climbed ridges, but mostly the elevation of the trail continued a gradual drop.

At one wide meadow, Teresa pointed to a large mountain they could see to the south.

"That is the mountain over Las Vegas," she said.

Buck looked down to the south where the hills opened up and framed the larger mountain. Buck remembered the rocky face on the north and east sides overlooking Las Vegas, but he would not have recognized it if Teresa did not point it out to him.

"It still seems so far away," Teresa said. "But I remember when Red and I came into the mountains we made it from Las Vegas to Rociada in one day. We camped at Rociada that night."

"We won't make it there today," Buck said.

"No. Red and I left early in the morning."

"Tomorrow, though," Buck said. "We'll be there tomorrow."

Teresa gave a noncommittal nod.

"If Rusty Hale does not catch us first."

Buck gave a touch with his heels to the mare's sides.

"You use that scattergun if you need to," he said. "Just point in the right direction and pull both triggers."

Teresa touched the butt of the gun where it stuck out of the scabbard to see how easily she could reach it. "I'm not afraid to use it," she said.

Buck glanced back over his shoulder.

Here, where the trail rolled with the hills and was heavily wooded with pines and juniper, it was harder to see if someone was coming after them than it would have been in the valley.

"He might catch us up without us knowing he's there," Buck said. "He'll be delayed some in getting his horse saddled. Who knows what he'll do with his dead brother. Maybe just leave him in that hallway for someone else to deal with. But sooner or later he's going to be coming for us."

Even through the woods the trail to Las Vegas was wide and easy to find. Though they'd not seen any travelers on the trail, Buck was sure the road saw daily travel.

"Maybe we'll ride through the night," he said. "I think there should be enough moonlight, and the trail is worn enough. We should be able to ride without losing the way."

Teresa sighed heavily. The thought of staying in

the saddle through the night exhausted her. She seemed to hurt all over, and she only wanted a soft bed and to not have to sit in a saddle or walk.

The trail opened up into a long, wide meadow that sloped gradually for some distance to a small creek. They forded it easily and followed a slightly steeper slope back into the woods and up to the top of a ridge.

At the ridge, Buck checked their backtrail. It was the first time since they'd left the big valley that he'd had a good, clear view of the ground they'd already covered.

"Ride on a ways," Buck said to Teresa. "I'll catch you up in a minute. I just want to watch behind us for a bit."

He sat the horse in the shade and took a drink from his canteen. He let the mare wander over to a patch of clover.

Teresa rode on forward and was soon out of sight.

Buck took his hat from his head and wiped his forehead on his sleeve. It was not overly hot, but the sun in the meadow had warmed him quite a bit. Now, though, in the shade of the trees, the easy breeze was chilly. The smell of the pines was pleasant and reminded Buck of home. It was a clean, fresh smell, foreign in Santa Fe.

Buck had been thirty minutes watching the backtrail and was ready to give up the wait, but then he saw two men ride into the meadow.

They were taking it easy on their horses, probably because they'd already ridden them too hard.

Buck did not doubt that it was Rusty Hale and the younger man he'd seen with them before.

He sat just one moment longer. He considered dismounting and attempting to ambush them right here. He could hide inside the tree line and wait for them to begin to the rise up the slope, but in the end Buck decided he would not have an ideal shot until they were too close.

Now he tugged the reins against the horse's neck and gave the mare a touch with his heels.

He ran the horse at a gallop to catch up to Teresa, and he was pleased to see that she had made good distance.

When he caught her she had already come down off of the ridge and into another meadow, thick with tall grass and weeds. A hillside to their left was covered in large sandstone boulders, and a creek cut across their path halfway down the wide field. The creek was very narrow and rocky, and though it was clear and cool water, it did not run as fast here as the creeks they had crossed at higher elevations.

Buck quickly took in all he could see. To their right, the creek cut a thick and narrow canyon, heavily wooded at the front.

On the other side was the hill with large sandstone boulders. There was not overhanging cliff on the hill, and farther up the pines wrapped around the top.

"We can make a stand here," Buck said.

Buck looked around one more time and satisfied himself that this was the right place. At least, right enough considering that they were now running out of time.

"Follow me to this canyon," he told Teresa.

"Did you see them?" Teresa asked. "Are they coming?"

"Damn near here," Buck said curtly, taking the lead of the pack horse and hurrying off the trail and down toward the canyon.

They cut out across the meadow and followed the creek bed down into the narrow canyon. Trees above and the undergrowth below gave the canyon a heavy cover where Rusty Hale would be unlikely to see the horses. The stream cutting through the canyon made enough noise as it flowed over rocks that if the horses snorted or blew they might not be heard. But the thing about the canyon that made Buck decide on it was the narrow space between the sandstone walls. If Rusty Hale came for Teresa inside that canyon, there would be nowhere to go when she pulled the triggers on the scattergun.

Buck climbed down off of the mare and helped Teresa down.

Working quickly, he picketed them deep in the canyon.

"You'll stay here with the horses," Buck said. "You'll be on your own here."

"Where will you be?" Teresa asked.

"I'm cutting over to the other side of the canyon. If I'm going to shoot it out with them, I don't want to be near you when it starts."

Buck took his box of cartridges for the Henry and put it inside his shirt. He looked around the canyon. Despite the growth of trees and brush, Teresa would be able to see the meadow, or most of it, from inside the canyon. Her view was obstructed some. But no one would be able to come into the canyon without her seeing.

"You've got a good position here," Buck said. "If they come for you, you use that shotgun. Get down behind that rock there and wait for them. When they come, let them get inside the canyon. Don't forget to cock back both hammers. And when they're close enough, let loose with both barrels. If they get me but don't find you, they'll keep going down the trail toward Las Vegas. If that happens, you go back to Rociada and find someone there who will help you."

Buck turned to leave, but Teresa caught him by the wrist.

"Don't leave me alone," she said.

"I ain't gonna leave you alone," Buck said. "But I am going to see to it that you and your baby come down out of these mountains safe."

He patted her hand on his wrist, and then gently lifted her fingers so that his arm was free.

Buck slid the Henry rifle out of its scabbard.

Once more Teresa stopped him. She stood up on her toes and leaned in toward his face, and she touched her lips to his cheek. It was rough with stubble from so many days not shaving.

"You're a good man, Gideon Buckner. I suppose you're the best man I've ever known."

Buck touched his hat.

"Thank you, ma'am. Now I've got to go do a job."

Buck started to leave her, but then he stopped and looked back at Teresa.

"If this thing don't go right for me, you get yourself back to Las Vegas. Dig up that money, and go on back east and raise that baby. Raise that baby to never know his daddy was an outlaw, and raise him to be a good man."

- 13 -

The young deputy hurried out across the meadow, running toward the rocks away from the canyon. If he was killed or injured, Buck did not want to be anywhere near Teresa where Rusty Hale might find her.

As he crossed the meadow at a run, Buck scanned the terrain for the right place. The sandstone boulders in the meadow were all too small for him to hide behind if he was standing. He would have to squat or lay prone.

He saw ahead of him and up the hill a short way a group of three larger boulders and decided that was the place. The boulders were within easy shot from the trail.

Buck knew he would not have to wait long. The riders would be upon him in a matter of minutes. He found that he now had fewer reservations about staging an ambush. Having done it once, it seemed like a small thing to do it again. If anything, Buck was more determined that he should finish off both riders.

He wanted this thing to end now.

The trail dropped down off the ridge and out of the tree line in a curve that went into the meadow. A large juniper bush blocked the view of the trail as it came out of the tree line, so the first look Buck had of the two riders was as they came around the curve. There was no question that it was Hale and the boy who'd been riding with the Old Bunch. Rusty Hale's arm was still bandaged from where Buck had winged him on the Pecos trail. They had left their remuda. Buck assumed the other horses were all back at Rociada.

With his hat on the ground beside him, Buck tried to make himself small behind the rocks, exposing just enough of himself to see the two riders.

They were watching the sign on the ground, and Buck realized the tracks would lead them directly to the canyon where Teresa and the horses were hidden.

They'd shown no sign of realization that they were being watched, and they rode into easy range. Even though he'd not yet raised up his rifle, Buck knew his first shot would kill one of the men, the same as he knew when he had a bead on an elk or a deer.

His breathing was steady. His hesitation was that he did not have a good shot at Rusty Hale. The younger man was riding with outlaws, but Buck had never seen him put a hand on a gun. He'd not seen him do anything but run the spare horses for the Old Bunch. And shooting him just to have a shot at Rusty Hale felt like cold-blooded murder.

The younger man was between Hale and Buck, and if he did not move or they did not alter their pace, Buck was going to have to kill the younger man first. For a host of reasons, the lawman did not want to do this.

They were nearing the place where Buck and

Teresa left the trail. In a few moments they would know something was amiss and be more alert.

Buck made a decision.

He let out a slow breath to fortify himself for what he intended to do, and then he stood up from behind the rocks. As he stood, Buck brought the rifle up to his shoulder.

"Throw up them hands," Buck shouted.

The two riders jumped in their saddles and turned their attention to Deputy Marshal Buckner.

"Put them hands in the air now, boys, or I'll shoot both of you out of your saddles."

Buck wasn't sure what he expected. Maybe they would go for their guns or maybe they'd do as they were told. But he was ready to shoot if they didn't put their hands up.

"I mean it," Buck said. "I'll kill you both."

That's when Rusty Hale leaned forward toward the younger man in the saddle beside him.

With a sudden and great push, Hale knocked the boy from his saddle.

The boy toppled and the horse bolted, all at the same time. But the boy's foot was stuck in the stirrup, and he began to bounce off the trail as the horse galloped away.

The surprise of it made Buck look away from his target, and Rusty Hale rolled down out of his own saddle, drawing his six-shooter as he went.

Buck turned back, trying to get a sight on Rusty Hale. But now Hale's horse was in the way, and Hale was making a run into the meadow.

Buck let out a curse and leapt over the rocks, running to get a position where he could shoot.

Buck fired off a shot that missed, but not by much.

Rusty Hale twisted and shot back. The bullet went well wide, careering into the trees far behind Buck.

Buck fired another shot just as Rusty Hale slid to the ground behind a sandstone boulder, but Hale yelped in pain, and Buck knew his shot had told.

"Throw out your gun, Hale," Buck shouted at him. "You're done here. This is over."

Hale's response was to lift himself over the boulder and snap off another shot. There was some aim behind this one, and the bullet hit Deputy Buckner in his left elbow as it jutted out, steadying his rifle.

Buck let out a howl of pain. His entire upper arm from elbow to shoulder felt like it had been shot right the hell off, and he was surprised when he looked down and saw his left arm still hanging limp by his side.

The pain was immense, and Buck's mind seemed to flash white hot lightning. He couldn't even remember how to breathe. Stunned and in terrible pain, Buck didn't move. He just stood where he was.

"What's the matter, deputy?" Rusty Hale called from behind the safety of the boulder. "You've been shootin' up all my friends, but you don't seem to like it much when you're the one getting shot."

Buck couldn't focus on the words. He was choking on air and trying to force himself to breathe it. Quick breaths that seemed to stick in his throat were all he could manage.

Now Rusty Hale stood up and began walking toward Buckner.

The threat to the last remaining member of the Old Bunch was gone. Buckner still held the Henry rifle in his right hand, but the barrel was pressed against the ground as the young deputy marshal from Santa Fe used the rifle to help him keep his feet on the ground.

Through the flashes of blinding pain, Buckner tried to focus on where he was. Tears were welling in his eyes, and he knew he didn't want to cry. He felt very small, like a child, trying to hold back the tears when his daddy died. He knew he had to be brave for his brothers and sisters, for his mother.

Thinking on his mother, Buckner remembered the woman who also called him Gideon, now hidden in a canyon. And through the pain he remembered a promise to protect her that brought him here.

He lifted up the heavy Henry rifle with one hand and squeezed the trigger. The big gun jerked in his hand and he stumbled backwards, dropping the rifle to the ground. Whatever happened to the bullet, it did not hit the man slowly walking toward him.

"You killed my brother today," Rusty Hale said. "I swore the sun wouldn't set on this day without me getting revenge. And look at this – it's still light outside."

Hale held his hands out wide to show the sunlight. His six-shooter was held casually.

Buck still fought to catch his breath. His mind was beginning to work again, but his left arm was useless. He searched the ground for the dropped rifle and found it at his feet.

Buck dropped down to one knee and picked up the rifle.

He struggled to raise it up. Rusty Hale was still some distance away, and Buck couldn't aim the gun. He laid the barrel across his knee and then worked to find the strength to lift it.

He held out straight in front of him.

The front sight wobbled, unsteady on its target.

Buck pulled the trigger and closed his eyes expecting the shot.

But the trigger didn't move and the gun didn't fire.

"You got to use the lever to cock them repeaters," Rusty Hale laughed.

"I ain't never been shot in the elbow before," Hale said. "That must hurt. You ain't even thinking right."

Buck struggled to his feet and stumbled backwards. He pressed the barrel of the gun to the ground, bent over it to hold it steady with his stomach, and then he worked the action on the lever. He raised up the gun again, and the barrel danced a jig to the music of Rusty Hale's laughter.

"Take your shot, boy," Rusty Hale said. "You can't even hold it to shoot straight. Take your shot."

Buck pulled the trigger again and the hammer fell on an empty chamber. The gun was jammed from the dirt that went in through the open ejection port.

Buck stumbled again and fell heavily, dropping the rifle as he hit the ground.

"What's the matter?" Rusty Hale asked. "You

outta cartridges or did your rifle jam on you?"

Deputy Buckner scrambled to get back on his feet, but he could only get himself to one knee.

He still could not catch a good breath.

Rusty Hale stopped walking toward Buckner and raised up his six-shooter. He took a sight and fired. The six-shooter spit out a puff of white smoke and the bullet smashed into Buck's shin.

Buck toppled over onto the ground, and when he hit the ground the box of bullets he'd stuck in his shirt spilled out all around him.

The fresh pain was so intense that Buck wretched, choking on the dirt and spit on his lips. Those tears welling in his eyes spilled over.

His cheek was pressed against the ground, and Buck looked through clouded eyes. He could barely see farther than a foot in front of his face. He was losing blood and felt weak. But there were brass cartridges gleaming in the sun all around him. Buck reached for one, missing it and coming up with a handful of dirt. But he moved his hand in the dirt until he found the cartridge.

His left arm was useless, and now his left leg was busted from where the lead ball smashed into his shin.

Deputy Buckner rolled onto his right arm, clutching that bullet in his hand, and he pushed himself up and fell over so that he was sitting on his butt. His left leg stretched out in front of him, just as useless as his left arm.

With the cartridge pinched between his forefinger and thumb, Buck reached out for the Henry rifle.

"It's jammed, remember?" Rusty Hale said. "It ain't gonna do you no good."

Buck nodded. His eyes drifted over to the canyon. He could not see Teresa in there, but without making a coherent thought, he prayed that she would survive this even if he did not.

"Leave the woman," Buck whispered, pulling the Henry to him.

"What's that boy?" Rusty Hale asked in mocking tones. "I can't hear you."

"Leave the woman alone," Buck said again.

With the Henry in his lap, Buck raised up his right knee to hide what he was doing.

"When she tells me where the money is hid and I'm done killing her, that's when I'll leave her alone. Now, you tell me where she's at."

"Back to the village," Buck said. "Rociada. She doubled back."

Hale laughed. He was nearer now.

Without looking at the gun, Buck felt for the ejection port. Then he pushed the cartridge down into the empty chamber. It was a trick Rick Compton taught him. A jammed Henry rifle becomes a powerful single-shot rifle if you load it through the ejection port.

Buck cocked back the hammer on the Henry.

"That ain't gonna help you, boy," Rusty Hale said with a grin. "Remember? It's jammed."

Buck laid the barrel on his raised up knee. The angle was too awkward to try to aim, but Rusty Hale was standing six feet away now.

"Throw down your gun," Buck said.

Rusty Hale laughed. "Like hell."

The last surviving member of Red Hogan's Old Bunch lifted his six-shooter toward the deputy marshal just as Gideon Buckner squeezed the trigger on the Henry.

The hammer dropped and the brass receiver spit flame and smoke as the bullet smashed heavy into Rusty Hale's chest.

Before Rusty Hale's body hit the ground, the Old Bunch was all dead.

- 14 -

    Gideon Buckner collapsed onto the ground. He was weak and bleeding. His left arm and left leg were mangled and useless. His brain gave up trying to fight unconsciousness, and Buck passed out.

    The younger man who rode with the remnants of the Old Bunch was flung free of the stirrup when the horse had run twenty yards. He was stunned and shaken but had gotten his senses back after the pounding.

    He was missing a boot – it had gone on down the trail with the horse, and his gunbelt had come aloose and was in the dirt back up the trail.

    He saw the shootout and watched in horror as his older brother Rusty was shot dead by the deputy marshal. Dick and Rusty – Jamie Hale looked up to his two older brothers all his life, and he never did believe a lawman was made who could kill them. And now, both in one day, gunned down by the same lawman.

    Jamie Hale's older brothers refused to ever let him ride along with them. But they had said this was going to be different. They were just going to ride into the mountains to see an old friend. Maybe kill him. And get what was theirs.

But it had all gone wrong. The new members of the Old Bunch were both dead. One shot on the Pecos trail. The other shot on the ridge dividing west and east on the mountain. And now the old members, Rusty and Dick – the last of the Old Bunch – they were dead, too.

Jamie limped up to his gun. His face and arms were cut all to hell from the horse dragging him, but he understood why Rusty pushed him out of the way.

Jamie picked up the gun by its grip, thumbed off the leather thong on the hammer, and then he slung the gun a couple of times until the holster and gunbelt slid away.

He walked with determination and purpose, his eyes fixed on the deputy marshal.

"Rusty!" Jamie called. His brother's body did not stir. "Rusty? Is you killed?"

The deputy marshal looked dead, too, but Jamie Hale was going to make damn sure of it. That deputy had killed off everything in this world that mattered to Jamie, including his dreams of one day riding with the Old Bunch. Dead or not, Jamie Hale was going to put lead in that deputy.

He limped up the hill. His leg felt like it had been jerked right out of his hip, but he kept going.

He never saw the woman emerge from the canyon with the double barrel shotgun, and he did not see her running up behind him.

He stopped for just a moment at Rusty's body, but

there was no question. Rusty's eyes were open in eternal surprise. His chest did not rise and fall. Rusty Hale was dead, and Jamie did not linger over his body.

The brother of outlaws instead limped forward to the lawman. His eyes were shut, but his chest rose and fell. He was still alive, still breathing. And Jamie Hale took some pleasure in knowing he was going to at least be able to avenge his brothers.

The youngest Hale boy cocked back his six-gun and leveled it at the deputy marshal.

He shut his eyes and squeezed the trigger, and the bullet opened up a hole in Gideon Buckner's stomach.

Jamie Hale opened his eyes and looked at the deputy's chest as it rose and fell again. Blood was pumping out of his abdomen. The deputy's eyes opened up and he groaned at this new pain that swirled in and mixed with all the others.

Jamie cocked back the hammer.

"You done for them, and now I'll do for you," Jamie Hale said.

He stopped and turned, though, because he'd heard a skidding in the dirt, and he was just in time to see the two open barrels of the scattergun raise up level with him. Jamie never even had a recognition of the woman behind the gun. He just saw those two barrels.

Teresa Hogan pulled both triggers and the big gun sounded like thunder as its pellets shredded the youngest Hale boy.

The kick of first the one barrel and then the other almost tumbled Teresa backwards, but she held her footing. Jamie Hale seemed to disappear in front of her as the two loads of shot spun him like a top and he crumpled to the ground.

She threw the heavy gun away and fell on her knees beside Gideon Buckner.

She put her hands over the wound leaking blood from his abdomen, but the blood just pooled up between his fingers.

"Buck?" Teresa said. "Buck, can you hear me?"

"Safe?" Buck whispered, but blood began to leak from his mouth, and Teresa could not understand.

"What?" she said.

"Safe?" Buck said again. "Promised."

"They're both dead," Teresa said. "They're both dead. You kept your promise Buck. I'm safe."

She did not think he could see her.

She kept one hand on the wound, trying to force the blood to stay where it belonged. She put her other hand in his hair, stroking his hair.

"You kept your promise, Buck," Teresa said again.

"Don't leave me," Buck said.

Teresa kissed his cheek.

"I won't leave you," she said.

He made a small noise in his throat, and then Teresa let out a quiet whimper when she realized that Deputy Marshal Gideon Buckner's time on this earth was done.

- 15 -

The train rolled into the station with a lurch, a cloud of steam, and squealing brakes.

From the window in her car, the woman who called herself Teresa Buckner had watched the approaching town with wide eyes.

"It's all so different now," she said. "I cannot even recognize it. None of this was here. I don't even know if I can find the old plaza."

The young man in the seat beside her watched his mother with curiosity. He'd never seen her like this before. Since they'd left the station at Topeka, she'd seemed to have a mix of trepidation and even sadness.

"Mama, are you sure you want to do this?"

Teresa Buckner pressed her hand against her son's face. She saw sometimes flashes of a man she remembered in his physical features, but it was not the man he knew as his father.

"Yes, Buck," she said. "I'm sure I want to do this."

Outside on the platform they found a man with a buggy to drive them to the Plaza Hotel.

"You be stayin' long?" the man asked as he drove the mule up the hill.

"Just a couple of days, sir," the young man said.

Teresa turned in her seat to look at the big Atchison, Topeka & Santa Fe train depot.

"It is hard for me to imagine that this is here," she marveled. "Everything is so different."

"You been to Las Vegas before?" the man driving the cart asked.

"I've never been here before. But my mama is from here, and my pa is buried here. I've come to meet him."

The man looked sideways at Buck. "Never met your pa?"

"He was a deputy marshal from Santa Fe. He was killed by outlaws."

"Sorry to hear that," the cart driver said.

"How long's it been since you've been here?" he asked Teresa.

"Nineteen years," Teresa said. "When I left Las Vegas, there was only the stagecoach. No train. No depot. And none of these buildings."

Teresa's eyes were wide with astonishment. Little Rock, what had been home for the last twenty years, had plenty of two and three story buildings down on Main Street and Louisiana Street. Along the river there were big factories and markets and St. John's College. Little Rock was laid out in a grid pattern with square streets and avenues. It was bustling just like any eastern city. So it wasn't the size and numbers of the buildings that amazed her, but to find them here in Las Vegas. And the wide avenues, all straight and crossing each other at regular square intersections. The Las Vegas that Teresa Buckner remembered was the small plaza with winding roads going off in any direction.

"This is New Town Las Vegas," the cart driver said. "Probably where a woman like you should be staying anyway, instead of at the Plaza. The Plaza is Old Town. Mostly Spanish in Old Town."

Teresa frowned at him.

"My people were Spanish," she said.

The man nodded. "Yes, ma'am. I reckon. But you've got money. Ain't a lot of money in Old Town anymore."

Teresa looked at Buck's suit. A fine suit fit for a young man who was apprenticing as a lawyer and taking classes at the college. And her dress was beautiful, and expensive. She realized how out of place they must look.

"My husband is buried in the churchyard at Our Lady of Sorrows," Teresa said curtly.

The carriage driver, feeling he had offended her, drove on in silence.

They checked in at the hotel. Teresa went up to her room to freshen up, and Buck sat on the front walk of the hotel waiting for his mother.

The Old Town was dirty and felt poor. Most everyone was of Spanish descent, like his mother. Old Town lacked the bustle of New Town. There were not carts hurrying this way and that. But a drunken man slept on a bench inside the gazebo in the center of the plaza across from the hotel.

After some time Teresa joined her son. She had changed clothes into a more modest dress, but it was still obviously new and much finer than anything the other women on the street wore.

Teresa looked around the plaza.

"Up this way," she said. "I have not forgotten."

They walked up a hill with a heavy slope.

"Are you okay to walk all this way?" Buck asked, taking his mother's elbow and helping her.

"You would be amazed to know how much walking I have done in these mountains," Teresa said.

The church was almost immediately in view as they left the plaza, its big, red-stone edifice still very prominent.

Many stones had been added to the churchyard in the years since she had left, but after some time, Teresa found the right one.

She reached out a hand and touched the cool rock surface.

"'Gideon Buckner,'" Buck read. "It's very strange to read my own name on a tombstone."

"What does that say under it?" Teresa asked, though she knew the answer. She wanted to hear her son say it.

"'A good man.'"

The boy stood quietly for a long time.

"You have earned his name," Teresa said. "All I

wanted was to raise you to be the kind of man who could live up to that name. And you have done it. No mother could be more proud of her son than I am of you."

Teresa patted the cool stone, and then she squatted down and pressed her lips against it.

"I've never told you the whole story, and it's not important that you know all the details. But this man died so that I could live, and so that you could live. He gave his word and he kept it, even though it cost him his life."

Buck stared at the inscription on the tombstone and tried to feel his connection to the man beneath it. In his heart, he did feel it, and the feeling was pride.

"You must have loved him very much," Buck said.

"More than you can know," Teresa said. "In all my life, I had never known another man like him. A man so polite and so honest. And he was brave, as you must be able to imagination. He stood up to some of the worst outlaws in this territory at that time. They were men who massacred an entire posse, and Gideon Buckner faced them to save me. I've never known another man who came close to your father."

Buck put his finger tips on his mother's shoulder when he saw the tears in her eyes.

"He did it to save you?" Buck asked. "You've never told me that before."

And then a thought occurred to him.

"Were you there when he was killed?"

Teresa nodded.

"It was in the hills not far from here," she said. "We were trying to get back to Las Vegas, and we were being hunted by these men."

"Why?" Buck asked. "Why were they hunting you?"

Teresa shook her head.

"It is not important. I knew something that they wanted to know. And they were going to do whatever they had to in order to make me tell them what they wanted to know, and then they were going to kill me. It was that simple. But your father protected me. He protected us – I was pregnant with you. He was killed saving us both."

She started to stand, but she found her legs had become suddenly weak.

Buck took her by the elbow and helped her to her feet.

"Are you okay?" he asked.

"The train ride was too long, and then the walking," she said. "I'm fine, though."

She took a step back where she could better see the market.

"'A good man,'" Teresa said. "We never talked about it, but I think it was important to him that you have his name. You are the fourth Gideon Buckner that I know about. Your father's father was also a lawman. He was killed in a shootout with a horse thief. And his father, who was also Gideon Buckner, he raised your father. Taught him to hunt and taught him about the woods and the mountains. Those lessons are why you and I are alive today."

Buck nodded, thoughtful. His mother had given him every advantage in Little Rock. He lived in a good home. He had decent clothes. He went to grade school and then college.

But Buck had always felt a little resentful when he saw the other boys he knew go hunting with their fathers, or visit their fathers in the places where they worked. Buck felt cheated. He wondered if his own father had felt cheated growing up.

"Maybe I should have married another man," Teresa said. "There were opportunities. When I was still young and pretty. And then you would have had a father to raise you. But this man who gave you your life and your name, he was the only man I wanted you to ever be like."

Buck chuckled.

"You've talked about him so much over the last nineteen years, I've always felt like I knew him. Maybe there were times when I was jealous of the boys who got to spend time with their fathers, but you never let me question whether or not my father was the –"

Buck stopped himself, searching for the words.

"You never let me question whether or not my father was a good man."

Teresa nodded.

"I wanted you to grow up to be a man who could carry a name like Gideon Buckner. And you do. You carry it well, Gideon. Just like your father did."

Teresa touched her son's cheek.

"And we've had a happy life," Teresa said.

"Yes, ma'am," Buck agreed.

the end

ABOUT THE AUTHOR

Robert Peecher is the author of more than a score of Western novels. He is former journalist who spent 20 years working as a reporter and editor for daily and weekly newspapers in Georgia.

Together with his wife Jean, he's raised three fine boys and a mess of dogs. An avid outdoorsman who enjoys hiking trails and paddling rivers, Peecher's novels are inspired by a combination of his outdoor adventures, his fascination with American history, and his love of the one truly American genre of novel: The Western.

For more information and to keep up with his latest releases, we would encourage you to visit his website (mooncalfpress.com) and sign up for his twice-monthly e-newsletter.

OTHER NOVELS BY ROBERT PEECHER

THE LODERO WESTERNS: Two six-shooters and a black stallion. When Lodero makes a graveside vow to track down the mystery of his father's disappearance, it sends Lodero and Juan Carlos Baca on an epic quest through the American Southwest. Don't miss this great 4-book series!

THE TWO RIVERS STATION WESTERNS: Jack Bell refused to take the oath from the Yankees at Bennett Place. Instead, he stole a Union cavalry horse and started west toward a new life in Texas. There he built a town and raised a family, but he'll have to protect his way of life behind a Henry rifle and a Yankee Badge.

ANIMAS FORKS: Animas Forks, Colorado, is the largest city in west of the Mississippi (at 14,000 feet). The town has everything you could want in a Frontier Boomtown: cutthroats, ne'er-do-wells, whores, backshooters, drunks, thieves, and murderers. Come on home to Animas Forks in this fun, character-driven series.

TRULOCK'S POSSE: When the Garver gang guns down the town marshal, Deputy Jase Trulock must form a posse to chase down the Garvers before they reach the outlaw town of Profanity.

FIND THESE AND OTHER NOVELS BY
ROBERT PEECHER AT AMAZON.COM

Made in the USA
Monee, IL
15 December 2025